P9-DMV-027

My Last Best Friend

My Last Best Friend

Julie Bowe

Harcourt, Inc.
Orlando Austin New York San Diego Toronto London

Many thanks to my agent, Steven Chudney, and to my editor, Kathy Dawson. And special thanks to my son, Eli (cow drawer extraordinaire), and to my daughter, Micah, for all the inspiration she provides.

www.HarcourtBooks.com

Library of Congress Cataloging-in-Publication Data
Bowe, Julie, 1962–
My last best friend/Julie Bowe.—1st ed.
p. cm.
Summary: After her best friend moves away, fourth-grader Ida May is determined not to make a new best friend, despite the efforts of a new girl in her class.
[1. Best friends—Fiction. 2. Friendship—Fiction. 3. Schools—Fiction.] I. Title.
PZ7.B671943My 2007
[Fic]—dc22 2006009244
ISBN 978-0-15-205777-0

Text set in Espirit Book
Designed by April Ward

First edition
A C E G H F D B

Printed in the United States of America

For my parents, Kris and Doris Henriksen,
my brothers Neil and Scott, and for my
sister, Carol, who long ago wished for a
little sister. I'm glad her wish came true.

My Last Best Friend

Chapter 1

I'm Ida May, and there's one thing I know. Fourth grade isn't fourth at all. *Fourth* means you've done something at least three times before. But fourth grade is nothing like third grade. Or second grade. Or first grade.

In fourth grade there is no more printing. There is only cursive. I hate cursive.

In fourth grade you are not allowed to add and subtract. You are only allowed to multiply and divide.

In fourth grade you're a baby if you still want to play with Barbies. Or if the Tooth Fairy still comes to your house. Or if you want your mother to walk you to the bus stop. Third grade is the last grade you can get by with any of that. Trust me.

In fourth grade you start to smell funny. So you

get your first stick of teen deodorant, even though you won't actually be a teen for at least three years. Your mom leaves it on your bed in a little brown paper bag. You rub some on. After five tries you finally hit your armpit. When your mom smells you, she smiles and starts talking about stuff like "body image" and "healthy attitude" and "girl power."

Fourth grade is when your parents worry you are spending too much time alone and insist you hang out with Jenna Drews, the daughter of your school's PTA president. Your mom is on the PTA and just assumes the president's daughter is a nice, friendly girl.

Jenna may have your mother convinced that she is the nicest girl in the whole town of Purdee, Wisconsin, but the truth is, when Jenna isn't busy saving the planet, she's busy being mean.

Just before school starts, your dad calls Jenna's mom and arranges to drop the two of you off at the movies. While you wait for Jenna to order her natural spring water to go with the organic popcorn she had to bring from home, you open your jumbo box of Choco-chunks and dig in.

Hmm... you say to yourself. *How many Choco-chunks can a person of average intelligence cram into her mouth without creating an emergency situation? Five? Ten?*

You do a little test. But just when you shove the eighth chunk into your mouth, you hear someone say, "Excuse me? What time is it?"

You look up and see a strange girl looking back at you. She's smiling at you with the kind of smile you don't see on a real person very often. The kind you see a little kid draw with a big fat crayon on a piece of white paper. The kind you have to force yourself not to smile back at.

Trust me, you don't want to get too close to big-crayon smiles. That's because people with big-crayon smiles don't stick around very long. They move away just when you've gotten used to the way their hand feels sticky when you hold it, or the way they hiccup when they talk fast, or the way they whistle by sucking in instead of blowing out, or the way they can touch their nose with the tip of their tongue.

I know because my last best friend, Elizabeth Evans, moved away. She was the only friend I needed because we liked all the same things. Messy art projects. Corny jokes. Mild cheddar cheese.

Oh sure, we promised to always be best friends and to write to each other every week, which I did even though I'm a better drawer than writer. But she never wrote back. I did get a birthday card from her, but it was really from her mother. I could tell by the cursive. And that's the last time I didn't hear from her.

"The time?" the strange girl says again.

You look at your watch, rearrange the Choco-chunks in your mouth, and say, "Fofurdy."

"Four thirty?" she repeats like you're speaking another language or something.

You nod, which apparently she is capable of understanding because she says, "Thank you!"

Just then Jenna arrives with her or*gag*ic food, sees the smiling girl, shoves you out of the way, and says, "Hi!" The girl says hi back, and right away Jenna starts asking her a million questions about herself. It doesn't take Jenna long to find out that her name is Stacey Merriweather, she just moved here, she's in the fourth grade, and she's planning to see the same movie you're planning to see—and, why yes, she'd love to sit with you, and oh, by the way, that's Ida May.

By the time the movie's over, Jenna has given Stacey one of her bracelets, taken her phone number, and quietly informed you that she will be going to the movies with Stacey next time, not you.

Then Jenna teaches Stacey a secret hand-signal thing to say bye, and Stacey does the signal thing to you, too, only you're holding half a box of Choco-chunks in your secret-signal hand. Choco-chunks fly all over the place when you try to do the stupid signal back. So, while Jenna marches off to inform the theater manager about the mess you made, Stacey helps you pick up Choco-chunks and says how nice it was to meet you and how happy she is that you'll be in fourth grade, too, and all the while she's smiling that big-crayon smile and you have to practically bite your bottom lip off not to smile back.

And instead of letting yourself snort in a secret sort of way when Stacey points to a squished Choco-chunk on the bottom of a large woman's shoe, you just say "See ya," and let Jenna yank you out the door.

Because if you don't get out of there right

away, it won't be long before you and Stacey are naming your socks and walking to the park backward and exchanging friendship bracelets that you promise never to take off even if they turn gray and start to smell like expensive cheese. And then you will promise to be best friends for the rest of your lives.

Or until one of you moves away.

Whichever comes first.

Chapter 2

Even though I wish that the first day of school will not come, it comes, anyway. And even though I wish that Elizabeth will be standing at the bus stop, wearing her CUCKOO FOR COCOA PUFFS T-shirt and mismatched sneakers, she isn't. The only people there are Quinn Kloud and his little sister, Tess. Quinn and Tess moved here last year.

It isn't long before Jenna arrives with her little sister, Rachel. Rachel stands with Tess. Jenna marches right past me and up to Quinn. "Ready for fourth grade, Quinn?" she asks.

Quinn shrugs. "I think it'll be better than third grade. At least I know some kids this year."

"Well, if it's friends you need, I can help," Jenna says. "I'm friends with everybody." Then she glances at me and adds, "*Almost* everybody."

Quinn just nods. Then he looks at me. "How about you, Ida? Are you ready for fourth grade?"

But before I can say "As ready as I'll ever be," Jenna butts in. "*Her*?" she says, giving me the once-over. "Looks to me like she's ready for *kindergarten.*" Then she pokes her thumb toward Tess and Rachel. "Don't you want to stand with your little friends, I-*duh*?"

I don't say anything. Jenna laughs and nudges Quinn. "I guess she can't take a joke," she whispers loudly.

Quinn just fidgets a little and pretends to be very interested in watching for the bus to arrive.

I watch, too, and wonder if Elizabeth already has friends at her new school or if she is also wishing that fourth grade wouldn't come.

I find an empty seat on the bus and sit down. I unzip my backpack and pull out my sketchbook. I open it up to a drawing of Elizabeth and me from last Halloween. Elizabeth was the front end of a horse. I was the back end. It was a great costume until we had to march in the Halloween parade at school. Jenna (who was dressed like an organically grown carrot) got in line behind us. She kept whacking me and shouting, "Giddyap, horsey!" I swear I still have bruises in places you can't see.

On another page there is a drawing of my family. I drew big smiles on me and my mom, and we have the words *ha-ha-ha-ha*... floating over our heads. That's because my dad has just told us a joke. Telling jokes is one of my dad's favorite things to do.

I turn the page again and see a drawing of my bedroom, including my bookshelf, which has about a hundred books drawn on it. I bet I've read every one of those books at least three times since Elizabeth moved away.

When I get to school, our new teacher, Mr. Crow, is standing outside our classroom door. He is saying hello and shaking hands with everyone. I start to walk up to him, but Jenna and another fourth-grade girl, Brooke Morgan, shove past me.

"Excuse us, I-*duh,*" Jenna says.

Brooke looks back at me and giggles.

Even though we have a new teacher and a new classroom, it doesn't take me long to figure out that some things haven't changed. Brooke Morgan, for instance. She is still the prettiest girl in our class. She has been the prettiest girl around for the past nine years. I know because ever since she was a baby she has gotten her picture in *The Purdee Press* sitting on Santa's lap. Every December a hundred kids line up in itchy red dresses or green clip-on ties, waiting for a turn to sit on the big guy's lap. But only one kid's picture gets on the front page, and it's always Brooke Morgan's. Even last year, when she was way too old for it. My dad says she has the kind of smile that could sell a million boxes of cereal.

I do not have a cereal-box smile. My smile is scrunched because my teeth are scrunched. My dad's an orthodontist, and he says I can have braces when all my baby teeth fall out, but based on the number of baby teeth I still have, I think I can pretty much count on having scrunched teeth at least until high school.

When I get inside the classroom, I realize that Mr. Crow does not believe in straight lines. That's because our desks are arranged in four clusters.

Apparently, Mr. Crow doesn't believe in alphabetizing either, because Rusty Smith's desk is right next to mine. Tom Sanders's desk is in my cluster, too, and so is Randi Peterson's. Randi Peterson is a girl, even though her name sounds like a boy's. She also acts like a boy, which means I have a lot of burping and ear picking to look forward to. But at least I don't have to sit with Jenna Drews.

Jenna probably thinks everyone wants to sit with her, but really everyone is afraid of her because she's so mean. In first grade, when our teacher showed us how to make minitornadoes by shaking up water, dish soap, food coloring, and vegetable oil in old pop bottles, Jenna made poor Tom Sanders *drink* his. Then she spun him around until his stomach must have felt like a tornado, because Tom turned as green as the food coloring we used.

In second grade, Jenna threatened to tell on Joey Carpenter for cheating on a math test unless he knocked a loose brick out of a school wall so it would collapse and we'd all get a long vacation while they built it again. Joey had to sneak a hammer and chisel to school. But it didn't work. Well, it sort of worked. He got caught, and when he told Ms. Stevens, our principal, it was all Jenna's idea, she got suspended for three days, which was sort of like a vacation for me.

Then, last year, Jenna made up new names for me and Elizabeth. I think she was jealous because we were best friends. She started calling us I-*duh* and Eliza*butt.* When you have a best friend, stuff like that doesn't bother you as much.

I sit down at my desk and glance over at Rusty. He doesn't seem to realize I'm there. Neither does Randi, who is busy shooting a crumpled paper ball at a hoop Rusty is making with his long, skinny fingers. Randi loves basketball. She even brings her own ball to shoot hoops at recess.

"Betcha can't make a three-point shot," Rusty says to Randi.

"Betcha I can," Randi answers and slides out of her desk. She takes a few steps back, narrows her eyes, and studies Rusty's freckled fingers. Then she lets the paper ball fly. Unfortunately, Tom Sanders arrives just as she shoots. The ball bounces off Tom's head and hits me in the nose.

Randi and Rusty crack up.

"What's a nose shot worth?" Randi asks Rusty.

"Four points!" Rusty says between laughs.

Randi turns her shaggy head to me. "Hey, Ida, let's go for *eight*!" she says, crumpling up a new paper ball.

Even though this is the first time Randi has ever invited me to join a game, I just say, "Um . . . no thanks," and turn my nose away.

As I do, I see that the new girl, Stacey Merriweather, has arrived and is sitting in a cluster near me, along with Jenna, Brooke, and Dominic Jordan. Dominic doesn't have much to say, but that isn't slowing down the girls.

"Did you move here because your parents got new jobs?" Brooke asks Stacey.

"Not exactly," Stacey says. "They, um . . . are news reporters. So they have to travel a lot to interview important people like, um . . . presidents . . . and kings . . . and queens, even," Stacey says.

Jenna lifts her chin. "My mother *is* a president," she brags.

"Not of a *country,*" Brooke says. "Just the PTA."

Jenna gives Brooke a look. But Brooke is too

busy staring at Stacey to notice. "I would love to meet a real queen," Brooke says.

Stacey clears her throat. "Well, I have. Twice. In fact, I'm pen pals with the queen of England."

"No way!" Brooke cries.

Stacey nods and fidgets a little.

Jenna's jaw tightens like she's sucking on a screw. "Well, if you and the queen of England are so *chummy,*" she says, "why aren't you staying with her while your parents are away?"

Stacey fidgets some more. "Because my parents made arrangements with my, um . . . aunt," Stacey says. Then she adds, "My *rich* aunt."

"Wow," Brooke says, her eyes expanding to the size of silver dollars. "It must be great to live with a rich aunt."

"Oh, it is," Stacey says. "Aunt Tootie redecorated one whole floor of her house just for me. I even have my own TV and computer in my bedroom."

"That's nothing," Jenna snorts. "I've had my own TV and computer since I was two."

"How about your own hot tub?" Stacey asks.

Jenna clamps her mouth shut. Brooke looks like she wants Stacey's autograph.

"How long do you get to live with your aunt?" Brooke asks.

I lean in, waiting for Stacey's answer. As I do, Stacey glances at me and smiles.

I do not smile back. I just pretend to be studying the classroom rules Mr. Crow is writing on the board while keeping one ear tuned into Stacey.

Stacey looks back at Brooke and Jenna. "Um . . . I get to live with my aunt until my parents are done traveling. Which will be a long time," she says.

"You must miss them while they're gone," Brooke says to Stacey.

"Yeah, I do," Stacey says, without fidgeting at all.

The bell rings and Mr. Crow starts taking attendance. I think about everything Stacey told Brooke and Jenna.

The more I think about it, the more I wonder if she was lying. That's because I saw her get dropped off at school this morning and she wasn't riding in any limousine. It was an old rusty van. And the woman driving the van did not look like a rich aunt. She looked more like a grandmother with pink curlers in her hair. Rich aunts never wear pink curlers in their hair. At least not in public. Plus, she kissed Stacey good-bye before she drove away. And Stacey even let her. Only grandmothers are allowed to kiss you in public past the second grade.

So that's why I'm sure Stacey isn't telling the truth.

But why would she lie?

Chapter 3

By the time Mr. Crow finishes taking attendance, and going over the classroom rules, and passing out our new books, it's time for our first recess. When everyone starts running outside, I realize I don't have Elizabeth to run outside with. Most of the boys head to the soccer field. Brooke is giggling with two other girls, Meeka and Jolene. Randi is playing basketball with Rusty and Quinn. Jenna grabs the last two swings: one for her and one for Stacey. That leaves me with nothing to do and no one to do it with. So I just wander around the playground by myself, pretending to be very interested in kicking rocks.

When we get back inside, it's time for silent reading, which, luckily, doesn't require any friends at all.

When it's time for lunch, Jenna grabs Stacey by the arm and starts dragging her off to the lunchroom. But Stacey glances at me and stops.

"What about Ida?" she says to Jenna.

"What about her?" Jenna replies.

Stacey turns to me. "Do you want to eat lunch with us, Ida?" she asks.

Even though I wish it was Elizabeth inviting me to lunch, it's a relief not to have to eat alone.

I nod.

Stacey smiles.

Jenna rolls her eyes. Then she links arms with Stacey and heads down the hall. I follow along.

When we get to the lunchroom, Jenna informs us that she has a cold lunch—bean sprouts on a whole wheat bagel, baby carrots, soy milk, and for dessert (yum-yum) carob brownies. So while she and her lunch go looking for a table, Stacey and I get in line for our UFOs (Unappetizing Food Options).

"Is the food any good?" Stacey asks.

"It's okay," I say. "If you don't mind food poisoning."

Stacey smiles her big crayon smile right at me.

"The food at my last school was so bad even the cook brought her own lunch."

"Oh, yeah?" I say. "Where *was* your last school?"

"Oh, not far," Stacey says, her voice trailing off. "Actually, technically, my last school was in my house. My parents wanted to spend more time with me, so they homeschooled me for awhile."

"But I thought I heard you say that your parents are always traveling because of their important jobs?"

"Oh, d-did I?" Stacey stammers. *Stammering* is what you call it when your mouth moves faster than your brain. "Well, they usually take me along when they travel, so they taught me while we were . . . um . . . on the road."

I nod like I believe her, but I raise one eyebrow like I don't.

"So, what do you like to do, Ida?" Stacey asks, like she's trying to change the subject or something.

"Oh, you know," I say. "The usual. I like getting up in the morning. Going to school. Going home. Going to bed. Stuff like that."

I am trying to sound as uninteresting as possible, but Stacey gives me a friendly laugh, anyway. "You're funny, Ida."

This conversation is going from bad to worse. Thankfully, the line moves forward and it's our turn to examine today's UFOs: turkey tetrazzini, buttermilk biscuits, and green beans.

"What'll it be, girls?" Mrs. Kemp asks, in her grumpy school-cook voice. Her pea-sized eyes blink at us over the thick rims of her steamy glasses.

Stacey and I look at the globs of turkey and noodles floating in gravy. We look at the rock-hard biscuits. We look at the soggy beans. Then we look at each other.

"Well?" Mrs. Kemp says. "Do you want hot lunch or not?"

Stacey and I gulp. Then we nod.

We get our food and Jenna waves Stacey over to a table where she is sitting with Brooke, Meeka, and Jolene. Stacey takes the seat across from Brooke. I sit next to Jenna.

"You're going to eat *that*?" Jenna says, wrinkling up her nose at my lunch. "*Disgusting,*" she says, looking at me. Then she looks at Stacey and smiles. "Be sure to bring a cold lunch tomorrow, Stacey. Then you can swap desserts with us." Jenna gives a glance to Brooke, Meeka, and Jolene.

"We swap lots of stuff," Brooke says. "Earrings, bracelets, shoes . . ."

"That's right," Jenna interrupts. "This necklace is Meeka's and this bracelet is Jolene's," she says, pointing at her neck and wrist. "Bring something to swap tomorrow."

"Su-ure," Stacey says. "I'll ask my gr— . . . my *aunt* if it's okay."

"Of course it's okay," Jenna says. "We do it all the time."

I scoop up some turkey tetrazzini on my fork and think about last summer when Elizabeth and I swapped flip-flops. We never got around to swapping them back before she moved away.

I'm right in the middle of remembering how much fun we had gluing pom-poms and plastic lobsters onto those flip-flops when I notice Jenna is glaring at me again.

"Wha?" I say through my turkey tetrazzini.

"You know what's *in* that turkey, don't you?" Jenna says back.

"Um, no," I say, swallowing. "I didn't realize there would be a quiz."

Jenna just shakes her head. "Horbones," she announces to the other girls. "Lots and lots of horbones."

"What's that?" Stacey asks, poking suspiciously at the food on her tray.

"That's the stuff that makes turkeys so *fat,*" Jenna says, giving me a glance. Then she starts to explain how *my* turkey spent its whole life inside a crowded pen eating horbones day and night with all the other unfortunate birds.

Three minutes into Jenna's lecture, I'm wishing I had warned Stacey not to show any interest in anything Jenna has to say. But then, I'm trying not to say much of anything at all to Stacey Merriweather.

I tune out Jenna's yakking, nibble on my rock-hard biscuit, and get a better look at Stacey.

She has pretty eyes and pretty, evenly spaced teeth. And pierced ears. Her hair smells the same way my mom's hair does after she gets a perm. I can't imagine having any friends if *I* smelled like that. Not that smelling the way I do has gotten me lots of friends. It hasn't.

Oh sure, I've had the regular kind of friends. The kind you wander around the playground with, making up excuses together for why you don't want to join the dodgeball game, when really you just don't want to look stupid when the red rubber ball smacks you in the face.

But that was before I met Elizabeth. She was the kind of friend who made it worth getting up and going to school every day just so I could sit by her on the bus and play with her at recess. The kind who told me secret things she never told anyone else. The kind of friend I never thought about having to say good-bye to until she all of a sudden decided to move away.

As I sit and watch Stacey listen to Jenna's description of her family's summer camping trip ("We had to brush our teeth with baking soda and pee in a hole. It was great!"), I think about Elizabeth and wonder if she's eating lunch at that exact same time, too. I wonder if she's as happy in her new school as Stacey Merriweather seems to be in hers. I want to say, *Excuse me, Stacey Merriweather, but don't you miss your old best friend at all?*

But before I have a chance to say anything, I

see it. A spitball. Right in the middle of my turkey tetrazzini.

I look up and see another one fly. This time it sticks in Stacey's curly hair.

I look around the lunchroom. Two tables away, Rusty Smith and two other fourth-grade boys, both named Dylan, are cracking up. A shredded napkin lies in front of Rusty. A straw is in his hand. I look at Stacey again. She's still eating and listening to Jenna talk, but I can tell by the way her eyes stop sparkling that she knows she's being used for target practice.

Then I see Rusty take aim again. And again.

After six direct hits, Stacey sets down her fork and quietly says, "Excuse me, ladies." She walks over to Rusty. He's so busy laughing with the Dylans that he doesn't notice Stacey putting her hand on his bony shoulder.

But he starts paying attention when she smiles at him and says in a sticky sweet voice, "You *like* me, don't you?"

Everyone within earshot turns and looks.

Rusty looks, too. "Huh?"

"You *do*!" Stacey squeals. "You *like me*!" Then

she puts her arm around him and practically sits on his lap.

Now everyone in the whole lunchroom is turning and looking.

Rusty peels Stacey's arm off his shoulder like it's a poisonous snake. Stacey puts it back. Everyone laughs. Then the Dylans start singing "Rusty li-ikes Staa-cey . . . Rusty li-ikes Staa-cey . . ."

Stacey smiles and scoots even closer to him.

By the third round of the song, the lunchroom sounds like the Mormon Tabernacle Choir. And Rusty's ears look as red as his hair. He wiggles out from under Stacey and bolts out the door.

I sit there, staring at Stacey Merriweather and wondering how a person with six spitballs stuck in her hair can do something like that.

Then Stacey gets up and walks back to our table. She sits down, picks up her fork, and finishes every last bite of her lunch.

Chapter 4

When I get home after school my mom is waiting for me in the kitchen with a plate of cookies. And a million questions.

"Do you like your new teacher?" she asks.

"He's okay," I say.

"What's he like?"

"Oh, you know. Nice."

"How about the kids in your class. Are they nice, too?" she asks.

I think for a moment. "Most of them," I say.

My mom looks pleased. "Who did you play with at recess?"

"Um . . . I ate lunch with Jenna."

"Well, that's good," she says. "But who did you play—"

Before my mom can finish her question I grab

three cookies off the plate and say, "Don't you have a student coming soon?" My mom teaches piano lessons in our living room.

My mom sighs and glances at her watch. "You're right. I have a piano lesson scheduled in a few minutes. We'll talk more about your day at supper, okay?"

I just nod and head to my room. A few minutes later the cookies are gone and some kid is plunking "If You're Happy and You Know It" on the piano.

I get up and shut my door. Tight.

When supper rolls around, I'm ready. As soon as my parents start asking me about my day, I stuff mashed potatoes into my mouth so all I can answer is "Mmm-hmm" or "Hmm-mmm."

The second I'm done with my third helping of potatoes, I ask to be excused.

"Are you sure?" my dad says. "I brought home chocolate ice cream for dessert."

Even though it's hard for me to turn down chocolate anything, I say, "I'm sure," and head to my room for the night.

When I get to school the next day it's apparent that standing up to Rusty Smith gets you magnetized or something. That's because fourth-grade girls are sticking to Stacey Merriweather like little bits of metal to a big shiny magnet. Jenna, Brooke, Meeka, and Jolene brush right past me as I walk down the hallway. They rush up to Stacey. Even Randi Peterson is taking a break from basketball to stick to her.

I stop and watch as they crowd together. Jenna is giving something to each girl. Probably money so they will keep pretending to be her friends. They are all chattering like chipmunks. Stacey is busy chattering, too. I bet she's telling them a bunch of new lies she made up overnight.

The only person drawing a bigger crowd than Stacey *Magnet*weather is Zane Howard. He's at the other end of the hall squeezing his neck until his face turns purple.

I swear, I will never understand boys.

"Ida!" Stacey calls to me. I look away from the boys and see Stacey's big-crayon smile shining like a supernova. I can feel its gravitational force pulling me in, but I dig my toes into the tile floor and hang on.

Stacey slips away from the other girls and walks up to me, waving a piece of purple paper. "Did you get yours?"

"Get my what?" I ask.

"Your invitation," Stacey says, handing me the paper. Unfolding it I read:

The next thing I know, Jenna is shoving an invitation into my other hand. "My mother says I have to invite every girl in the class. Even you, I-*duh*."

I look from the invitation to the crowd of girls. I see purple paper everywhere.

Jenna grabs Stacey's hand and pulls her away from me. And that's how Jenna and Stacey stay for the rest of the day. Stuck together.

When I get home after school I go straight to my bedroom. I toss my backpack on the floor and fall onto my bed, relieved to be somewhere soft and warm and familiar. I look at my sock monkey, George, who is lying on my pillow. George isn't particularly soft or warm, but he is familiar. He's been in our family since my dad was a kid.

I pull my invitation from Jenna out of my pocket and show it to George. "Everyone's going," I tell him. "Except me."

George just stares at me.

"Because," I say. "Sleepovers are stupid."

George takes time to think this over. While he's thinking I hear a knock on my door. A moment later my mom is peeking in.

"Hi, Ida! I thought I heard you come home. Can I come in?"

I slip the invitation under George and say, "Sure."

My mom sits next to me on my bed. "How was your day?" she asks.

"Fine," I reply.

"What did you do?"

"Oh, you know. The usual. Reading. Writing. Math."

"How about recess? Did you play with Jenna?"

"No," I say. "She was busy playing with the new girl."

My mom's eyes brighten. "The new girl?"

I fidget a little and nod. "Stacey Merriweather."

"Is she nice?" my mom asks.

"She's okay," I say, and fidget some more. Of course, George decides to fidget right along with me. It isn't long before Jenna's invitation is peeking out from under him.

"What's that?" my mom asks, pointing to the purple paper.

"Oh, it's just an invitation," I say. "To Jenna's sleepover. But I'm not going."

"Not going?" my mom says. "Why not?"

I just shrug and tuck the invitation back under George. "Jenna only invited me because her mom said she had to."

"Now, Ida, I'm sure that's not true."

"Yes it is," I say. "Jenna's mean. She only pretends to like me when you're around. I'm *not* going to her sleepover."

"But, Ida," my mom says. "You've hardly left this room since Elizabeth moved away. This party will be a chance for you to make some new friends."

"I don't need new friends," I say, and slide off my bed. "Besides, I like my room. And staying home with you. And Dad. And George. Plus, I'm busy with a new drawing." I grab my backpack and pull out my sketchbook.

My mom just sits there. Then she takes the invitation out from under George and looks it over. "Let's talk about this when Dad gets home."

"Fine," I say. "But I'm still not going." Then I open my sketchbook and start to draw.

As soon as my dad gets home, he and my mom start talking all quiet downstairs. I know because I'm pressing my ear against my bedroom door. A few minutes later, I hear my dad bounding up the steps, two at a time. I dive for my bed and give him a casual "Come in" as soon as he knocks.

My dad plops down on my bed, wearing his usual goofy grin. "Hi, Ida. Gotta joke for you," he says.

I sit up a little. "Let's hear it," I say.

"Knock, knock."

"Who's there?"

"Boo."

"Boo who?"

My dad frowns in a concerned sort of way. "Aw, Ida. Don't cry!"

I roll my eyes.

My dad laughs. "I know," he says. "It's not my best joke, but I thought it might cheer you up."

"I don't need cheering up," I say.

My dad's goofy grin trails away. "Yeah, you do, Ida. And Mom and I have decided you're going to the sleepover."

I jump off my bed and punch my fists into my hips. "But *I* don't want to go!" I shout.

My dad nods. "I know," he says, all calm. "But you can't keep moping around. We think making new friends is a good idea. Mom will call to let Jenna's mom know you'll be there."

I grab the closest thing to me, which is George, and throw him as hard as I can. George hits my dad in the chest and then falls in a gangly heap on the floor.

I fall to the floor, too.

My dad just sits there for a moment. Then he gets up and quietly closes the door on his way out.

I curl up into a tight ball, breathing hard and blinking fast so that no tears will be able to leak out.

Finally, I reach over and pull George to me.

"I'm sorry," I say.

Chapter 5

Friday morning my mom helps me pack my bag for the big sleepover. Pajamas, clothes, flashlight, hairbrush, toothbrush, toothpaste, deodorant. . . .

I want to bring George, but I know Jenna would do something mean to him. One time Elizabeth brought her favorite rag doll to school and Jenna stole it. Then she, Brooke, Meeka, and Jolene threw the doll in a Dumpster because they said it was old and smelly. I don't want George to end up in one of Jenna's recycling bins.

I spend most of Friday morning thinking about how much I don't want to go to Jenna's sleepover. But by the time lunch rolls around, all I can think about is—what is Stacey's real name?

I know, I know. You're saying, *Her name is Stacey.* And you're right. It is. But it isn't.

I guess I better try to explain.

It all started because our whole class was acting way more brainy than usual. We all got perfect scores on our first spelling quiz. Mr. Crow was so pleased he decided we deserved a reward.

"Howz' about we play a game?" he said. "It's called Fib."

Mr. Crow explained that each of us had to think of three things to tell about ourselves, but one of the things had to be a fib. "We'll try to guess who is fibbing about what," Mr. Crow said. "It'll be fun."

Mr. Crow started the game off by saying, "Three things about me are:

1. I was born in England.
2. I don't own a television.
3. My brother is a plumber."

Right away kids started waving their hands in the air. Everyone guessed that he was fibbing about not owning a television. But not me. I figured anyone with a ponytail as long as Mr. Crow's, who isn't a girl, probably spends most of his time reading really thick books instead of watching really stupid TV shows. Plus, he is always drinking tea, which means he must have been born in England since tea is pretty much all they ever drink over there. So I raised my hand and said, "You're fibbing about your brother."

"Good answer, Ida!" Mr. Crow said. "You are absolutely correct. My brother is a veterinarian, not a plumber."

"So that means you really don't own a television?" Jenna asked.

"That's right," Mr. Crow said.

"Weird," Jenna replied. Pretty much the whole class had to agree with that.

Next, we went around the room and took turns making up fibs. When it was my turn I said, "Three things about me are:

1. I have Dr. Seuss's autograph.
2. I want to be an artist when I grow up.
3. My dad wears Scooby Doo underpants."

Brooke guessed that I was fibbing about the autograph. Nope. That was true. My mom met

Dr. Seuss when she was a kid, and she gave me the book he autographed for her.

Tom guessed that I was fibbing about wanting to be an artist because nobody's ever seen my sketchbook.

"So that means you're fibbing about your dad wearing Scooby Doo underpants?" Stacey finally guessed.

"Yep," I said. "He only wears Bugs Bunny."

When I said that, Stacey laughed so hard I thought she might pee her pants.

After a few more kids told fibs, it was Stacey's turn. She said, "Three things about me are:

1. I like making new friends.
2. My favorite color is green.
3. My real name isn't Stacey."

Jenna guessed that Stacey was fibbing about her favorite color. Surprise, surprise. Even the boys knew that on account of practically everything Stacey owns is pink or purple. Jenna gave herself a round of applause for being right and then barged right into telling her fib.

But something *wasn't* right. Stacey said she

fibbed about her favorite color, which means the other two things were true. Then . . . what is her real name?

I don't know why I need to know her real name. I just do. But I don't want her to know that I want to know.

By the time lunch is over, I know what I have to do.

Instead of going straight outside for recess, I sneak back to our classroom. I pull a crumpled piece of paper and a half-chewed pencil from my desk. I think for a minute, and then I write:

So what IS your real name?
Signed,
A Girl

I toss the note on Stacey's desk. Then I race outside before anyone catches me sneaking around.

I kick rocks around the playground five times before I realize I made the stupidest mistake in the history of the world.

How is Stacey Merriweather supposed to answer my question when she doesn't know who is asking it? Will she get up in front of the whole class, wave my piece of crumpled paper in the air, and shout, *"What girl left this note on my desk?!"*

If she does, I will turn as red as Rusty Smith's hair. Then everyone will know it was me.

While I'm thinking this through, the bell rings, and I know I have to get that note before Stacey does.

I race into the school, barrel through a bunch of first graders, slip past the office, and tear down the hallway. It seems to take forever, but I finally zoom through our classroom doorway.

Then I freeze.

Stacey Merriweather is standing by her desk. She's tucking my crumpled piece of paper into her pocket.

I am toast.

"Excuse *me,* I-*duh,*" Jenna suddenly says as she shoves me through the doorway.

She shoves me so hard I trip over my feet and fall flat on my face.

Jenna looks down at me. "You should be more

careful," she says with a smirk. She steps over me and marches to her desk.

Stacey just stares at Jenna like she doesn't know what to say.

Everyone starts coming into the classroom, so I get up and slump to my desk.

Stacey walks over to me. "Are you okay, Ida?" she asks. "You'll still be able to go to Jenna's party, won't you?"

"I'm fine," I mumble.

"Because I really want you to go. And I'm sure Jenna didn't mean to knock you down."

"Yeah, and I'm an Olympic athlete," I say.

I squeeze my eyes shut until Stacey gets the hint and goes back to her desk. A minute later I hear Mr. Crow say, "Take out your science books, please." I take a deep breath and open my eyes. That's when my heart stops.

On the chalkboard, between next week's spelling words and today's math problems, I see it.

Anastasia

In curly cursive letters.

I blink my eyes and look again.

It's still there.

Anastasia

It's Stacey's name. Her real name. It has to be. The most amazing name I've ever seen.

Suddenly I realize Stacey isn't going to wave my note around and make me look stupid in front of the whole class.

She's keeping it a secret.

Our secret.

I don't dare look at Stacey. I don't want her to know I left the note. Or even suspect that I did.

So I keep my eyes straight ahead, staring at that amazing name. And it's a good thing, too, or I would have missed the other message.

Just before Mr. Crow erases the board, I see it.

In teeny-tiny print:

Girl: What's your real name?

Chapter 6

I spend the whole afternoon wondering what I should do. *Should I tell Stacey I left that note? Should I tell her my real name?* I keep coming up with the same answer.

No.

Even if I wanted to be her friend, which I don't, she's sticking up for Jenna, which means it's only a matter of time before she hates me, so what's the point?

I'm still thinking about this as we head out to the bus after school. Jenna organizes us into a jumbled line. She is in the lead. I bring up the rear.

The bus is crawling with kids by the time we climb on. Jenna takes command of the situation, maneuvering Stacey and Brooke through the obstacle course of knees and elbows. They pile into an open seat near the back. Randi plows through next, clearing a path for Meeka and Jolene. They squish into the last empty seat just behind the other girls.

I stand at the top of the stairs and look down the aisle, feeling like a fish who is about to be flushed.

"Quickly, now," the bus driver says to me. "Find a seat." She pulls on the long handle that's connected to the door, closing it with a snap.

I scan the sea of heads and backpacks.

I see some space near the front, where all the little kids sit. I plunge in and stop alongside Rachel Drews and Tess Kloud.

"Hi, Rachel," I say. "Can I sit with you?"

Rachel looks up at me, wrinkling her forehead into a question mark. "How come?" she asks.

"It's me," I say, forcing a smile. "Ida May. I'm going to your house for Jenna's sleepover."

The bus suddenly jerks forward and I have to grab the back of Rachel's seat to keep from falling.

"It's too squishy with three," Rachel says. Tess nods.

"Sit down!" the bus driver hollers at me.

I nudge myself onto the edge of Rachel and Tess's seat. They both complain, but I pretend I can't hear them.

The bus bumps along, and my legs begin to feel like they are going to fall off. At least it isn't a long ride to Jenna's house. I know where she lives even though I've never actually been inside.

When we get to the bus stop I hurry off and wait for the other girls. Rachel waits with me. When they finally pile out, Jenna links arms with Stacey. The other girls link up, too. "All for one, and one for all!" Jenna cries, as they march down the sidewalk together. Rachel and I fall in behind.

"You'll love my house, Stacey," Jenna says. "Everyone does." The other girls nod. "We can do whatever we want. My mom won't care. We can even stay up all night."

"Me, too?" Rachel asks.

Jenna shoots a look back at Rachel and me. "No *babies* allowed," she snaps.

As I listen to the girls making their plans for the night, I think about the last time I went to a sleepover, just before Elizabeth moved away.

All her toys had already been packed. So had most of the furniture. Even the bowls and spoons had been packed, so we pretty much just had to sit around on the floor and eat cereal right out of the box.

The longer I sat there and watched Elizabeth's mom and dad running around, rolling up rugs and carrying boxes out to the moving van, the more I wondered if maybe *my* parents were thinking about moving away, too. And then I started wondering if maybe they were packing up the beds and spoons at that very moment. In fact, when I got home in the morning maybe the whole inside of my house would be gone, including my parents.

The more I thought about that and the more I watched Elizabeth digging through the cereal box, the more I felt like crying. So I did. And when Elizabeth asked me what was wrong, I said my stomach felt funny. And when she held out a handful of sweaty purple marshmallows and said, "Eat these," I said, "No thanks," and threw up in her hand.

So Elizabeth and her mom drove me home real fast because they didn't want their van to smell like puke all the way to Albuquerque.

But the funny thing was, as soon as we got to my house I started to feel a lot better. I jumped right out of the van and ran up to the door. My mom opened it and I could see that all the furniture was still there, and that made my stomach sort of smile.

In fact, I felt so good I ran right inside.

And forgot to say good-bye to Elizabeth.

Chapter 7

As soon as Jenna opens the front door to her house we are attacked by a yippy ball of fur on four legs.

"Get down, Biscuit!" Jenna hollers. But Biscuit keeps jumping all over us like a Slinky gone bad.

Rachel finally gets hold of Biscuit and holds his trembling body tight so the other girls can pet him.

"I wish I had a dog," Stacey says, nuzzling in close to Biscuit and even kissing him on the nose.

"How come you don't got one?" Rachel asks.

"Um . . . my family is too busy traveling all over the world to take care of a pet," Stacey replies.

"Doesn't your aunt have a pet?" Meeka asks.

"Um . . . yes, five actually. Three dogs and two cats. But they're all show animals, so I'm not allowed to play with them," Stacey says.

"Wow, her house must be really big to have so many pets," Jolene says.

"Oh, yes," Stacey replies. "You might even call it a mansion."

"I bet it's not as big as my house," Jenna says. "But I guess we'll find out tomorrow."

Stacey suddenly stops petting Biscuit. "Tomorrow?" she says.

"Of course," Jenna replies. "When we take you home."

"Oh, um . . . I forgot about that. I mean, I forgot to tell you," Stacey says. "My aunt wants me to walk home . . . early. It's not far and she thinks I need the exercise."

Jenna frowns. "But—," she starts to say.

"I can't wait to see your room, Jenna," Stacey interrupts. She gives Jenna her biggest crayon smile.

Jenna lifts her chin. "Of course you can't," she says. "Follow me."

Rachel takes Biscuit outside. The rest of us gather up our stuff and follow Jenna through the house. It's big and airy enough to grow trees.

Strange paintings dot the mud-colored walls: scribbly flowers and crooked faces with four eyes and two noses. *I can draw better than that,* I say to myself.

Jenna's room is so sunny you'd think a cheerful girl lives there. Glow-in-the-dark stars and planets hang from the ceiling. Grass green rugs are scattered on the wooden floor.

I tap the hard floor with the toe of my sneaker. "How are we supposed to sleep on this?" I ask.

"Don't be stupid," Jenna says, dumping her school stuff on the floor and jumping onto her big bed. "Everyone knows you don't sleep at a sleepover."

Brooke giggles and joins Jenna on her bed. So do Meeka and Jolene. Randi shouts, "Monkey pile!" and dives on top of them. They all scream and bounce and giggle.

"C'mon, Stacey!" Jenna shouts.

"Ready or not, here I come!" Stacey cries. Then she turns to me and whispers, "I was wondering the same thing, Ida. About sleeping on the floor." She smiles at me. And dives onto Jenna's bed.

Just then Jenna's mom walks in carrying a plate of cookies. Her hair falls in two braids over her shoulders, just like Jenna's. She smells like oatmeal.

"Hi, Mom!" Jenna calls from the bed.

Jenna's mom smiles at all the bouncing girls. Then she notices me.

"Oh, hello, Ida," she says.

"Hello," I say back.

She holds the plate out to me. "Treat yourself to a homemade cookie, Ida. I'm sure you're used to store-bought."

I take one of the cookies off the plate and nibble it, even though I don't have much of an appetite. "Yum," I say.

Jenna's mom lifts her chin. "I'll give the recipe to your mother," she says. She takes a step toward Jenna's bed. "Girls? I have oatmeal cookies right out of the oven!"

"Thank you!" all the girls chime.

"Jenna, why don't you introduce me to your new friend?" her mom asks.

Jenna pulls Stacey out from the tangle of girls and says, "Pauline Drews, meet Stacey Merriweather. Stacey Merriweather, meet Pauline Drews."

Stacey giggles and waves to Jenna's mom. The other girls pull her back in.

Jenna's mom looks pleased. "Jenna, bring the girls down to the kitchen in a few minutes. I'm getting a craft project ready for you."

The girls keep bouncing.

Jenna's mom glances at me. "Here, Ida," she says, handing me the plate of cookies. "Give these to the girls when they're done playing."

I take the cookies, and Jenna's mom breezes out the door.

A minute later, Stacey bounces off the bed and over to me. "Can I have a cookie, Ida?" she asks, all bright and breathless.

"Help yourself," I reply. But just then Jenna shouts, "Wait, Stacey! You don't want those."

"Why not?" she asks.

"Because I have something better, don't I, girls?" She gives Brooke, Meeka, and Jolene a sly look. They bob their heads up and down, giggling.

Jenna jumps off her bed and reaches underneath. She pulls out a box that's filled with packages of store-bought cookies and candy bars. She dumps them on her bed. Brooke, Meeka, Jolene, and Randi dig in.

Stacey looks at me. "Do you want some chocolate, Ida?" she asks.

"Um . . . no thanks," I say, holding up my oatmeal cookie. "I'm good."

Stacey gives me half a smile and then joins the chocolate feast.

I set the plate of cookies on Jenna's dresser and walk over to her bed. I pick up one of the packages of cookies and look at the ingredients label. Then I look at Jenna. "I thought your family didn't believe in preservatives," I say.

Jenna snatches the package out of my hand. "Lighten up, I-*duh.* It's a party." Jenna takes a big bite out of a caramel candy bar. "And *don't* tattle to my mother about this," she says, shaking the candy bar at me. "If you tell her I'll . . ."

"You'll what?" I ask.

Jenna thinks for a moment. Then she narrows her eyes and licks caramel off her lips. "I'll tell everyone you peed your pants at my sleepover."

I glare at Jenna. "That's a lie," I say.

Jenna shrugs. "Maybe it is, maybe it isn't." She scans the other girls' faces. "Ida peed her pants at my sleepover, *right*?" she says.

Brooke, Jolene, Meeka, and Randi look at me. Then they look at Jenna. And nod.

I look at Stacey.

She glances away. And nods, too.

"See?" Jenna says. "It *is* true."

I storm out of Jenna's room and crumple against the wall in the hallway. I wish I had my sketchbook so I could draw a picture of my house, dive into it, and lock the door.

"That wasn't very nice, Jenna," I hear Stacey say.

"I was just joking," Jenna replies.

"Still," Stacey says. "You should tell Ida you're sorry."

I hear Jenna make a big sigh and slide off her bed. A moment later she's standing over me. "Please accept my apologies," she says loudly, so the other girls can hear her. She tosses a candy bar onto my lap. Then she leans over and whispers, "Don't be such a baby, I-*duh.*"

Chapter 8

It isn't long before all the cookies and candy have disappeared and Jenna is leading the way to the kitchen.

Jenna's mom has covered the kitchen table with newspaper. A pile of rocks is at the center of the table along with paints and brushes. Rachel is already sitting at the table, wearing a paint smock over her clothes. The smock is splattered with paint, and there is a paintbrush in her hand. Several rocks painted like bugs and butterflies are on the table around her.

Rachel looks up as we come into the kitchen. "We're painting rocks!" she cries.

"Duh, Rachel," Jenna says. "We're not blind."

Jenna turns to us and announces, "We collected these rocks on our summer vacation. Find one you like and paint it."

There aren't enough chairs for everyone, so I just stand next to Rachel. The girls start digging through the rocks. I start digging, too, even though all the paint and newspaper and brushes make me think of the messy art projects Elizabeth and I used to do. Which makes me miss her even more.

"That's an interesting one, Ida," I hear someone say.

I look up and see Stacey pointing at a rock that has fiddled its way into my hand. It doesn't look very interesting to me. Just an ordinary grayish color, flat on one side with a knobby bump on the other side.

"It looks like a humpback whale," Stacey says, taking the rock from my hand and turning it so that the knobby bump is on top. Then she moves it up and down in the air like it's swimming. "Maybe an enchanted whale . . . ," she adds in a dreamy voice, ". . . who rose from the depths of a magical sea in search of you, Ida."

"Huh?" I say.

Stacey just smiles and swims the rock back to me. "It's a nice rock, Ida. I like—"

But before Stacey can finish what she was

going to say, Rachel yanks on my sleeve, getting brown fingerprints all over it. "Look!" she hollers. "Biscuit!"

Rachel holds up a drippy brown rock in her equally drippy hand. The rock also has two drippy yellow dots that are apparently supposed to be eyes.

Jenna groans at her little sister. But Stacey looks at that mess of a rock and smiles. "It looks *exactly* like Biscuit," she says. Then she reaches over and takes the rock from Rachel. She paints *Biscuit* on the back while Rachel beams. *Beaming* is what you call it when your face just about splits open because of your big smile.

I know all about beaming. That's because Elizabeth was a great beamer. When she beamed, you just couldn't help beaming right back.

I do not beam at Rachel. I just stand there looking at all the rocks the girls are painting. Jenna's rock is carob colored with creamy speckles. She's painting wings and a beak on it. Brooke's rock is flat and squarish. She's painting it to look like a picture frame and says she's going to paint herself inside. Randi's rock is almost perfectly round. She's painting it to look like a basketball. Meeka and Jolene are painting matching flowers on their rocks. And Stacey finds two rocks that are the same shape and starts painting them like a pair of pink ballet slippers.

Jenna's mom comes over to see how we're doing. She notices my painted sleeve. "Jenna," she says. "Ida has gotten paint all over herself. Go get a clean shirt for her to wear while I wash this one."

Jenna's jaw drops. "One of *my* shirts?" she says.

"Yes, one of your shirts," her mom replies. "A large one."

Jenna pushes away from the table, grumbling.

"Never mind," I say. "I have an extra shirt in my bag."

Jenna sighs with relief.

I set down my whale rock and go upstairs to change.

When I come back to the kitchen everyone is gone except for Jenna's mom. "The girls went outside to play, Ida," she says, taking my painted shirt from me. She heads off to the laundry room.

I think about going outside, too. I walk over to the table instead.

All the painted rocks are sitting together at the center of the table, drying. My whale rock sits off to one side. I'm surprised to see it now has a tail, fin, and smiling face painted on it. *Stacey,* I say to myself.

Just then I hear a noise under the table. I bend down, expecting Biscuit to spring out and lick my face.

"Hi, Ida!"

It's Rachel.

"What are you doing under there?" I ask, pushing aside one of the chairs.

"Hiding," she says.

"From what?" I ask.

"That," she says, pointing past me.

I look in the direction she's pointing and see a coat tree by the kitchen door.

"You're afraid of coats?" I ask.

"Not coats," Rachel says, her eyes widening. "It's a monster."

"Yikes," I say.

Rachel smiles. "Quick, Ida! You'll be safe inside my castle!" She grabs my arm and pulls me under the table.

Rachel scoots over to make room for me. I sit down next to her and look around. "This is your castle?"

Rachel nods and pushes the chair back in place. She pretends to lock it with a key.

"Does that mean you're a princess or something?" I ask.

Rachel nods again. "Princess Penelope," she says. Then she leans in close and whispers, "It's my secret name."

"Don't worry," I whisper back. "I won't tell."

Rachel beams at me. "You need a secret name, too, Ida."

She reaches behind her back and then holds up an invisible crown. I lean over a little so she can put it on my head. "I crown you . . . Queen Cordelia," she says.

I sit up and pretend to straighten the crown. "How do I look?" I ask.

Rachel giggles. "Good," she says.

"Now what?"

"Now you guard the castle while I fight the monster."

Rachel pulls several rocks out of a pocket in her smock and shows them to me. "Ammunition," she says. Then she starts to unlock the castle door.

"Wait," I say. Rachel stops and looks at me. I pretend to sprinkle something over the rocks.

"What's that?" Rachel asks.

"Magic dust," I whisper.

Rachel beams again. Then she says, "Ida, you're a lot more fun than Jenna."

I give her half a smile. Then I sprinkle magic dust on her, too. "Be brave, Princess Penelope."

Rachel gives me a steady nod. "I will," she says. "Fighting monsters ain't for sissies."

She slips out of the castle. I close the door.

Then I sit back and watch her pelt rocks at the coat tree.

Fourth grade ain't for sissies either.

It isn't long before Princess Penelope returns to the castle, victorious.

"Want to have a celebration feast in my room, Queen Cordelia?" she asks.

"Sure," I say. "I've got nothing better to do."

Rachel crawls out of the castle. "Wait here, Queen Cordelia," she says. "I'll call you when the feast is ready."

"As you wish, Princess Penelope," I reply.

Rachel runs off.

I crawl out from under the table and walk over to the kitchen window. The girls are still outside, chasing each other around the house, screaming and laughing.

"Peasants," I say, using my most queenly voice. I guess getting a secret name changes the way you sound, too.

A secret name, I say to myself.

Suddenly, I have an idea. I don't have to tell Stacey it was me who left that note at school. I can tell her a secret name instead of my real name.

But what name?

It has to be amazing, like Anastasia.

It has to be . . .

Cordelia.

I walk back to the table. I pick up a paintbrush and write *Cordelia* on the back of my whale rock. Then I paint little stars around it for magic dust.

I hear the girls coming back inside.

I quickly turn the rock over and set it by Stacey's painted ballet slippers.

Then I smile.

A little, scrunched smile.

Chapter 9

When I get to school on Monday, I read the note I wrote to Anastasia again.

Dear Anastasia,

I can't tell you who I really am. But I am NOT Jenna Drews.

Thank you for not waving my other note in front of everyone.

I will be grateful if you don't wave this note in front of everyone, either.

Yours truly,

Cordelia

Simple, yet sincere.

I stuff the note back inside my pocket and wait for the sidewalk to clear. I don't want any snoopy second graders watching me sneak behind the school.

And I need to sneak, because I have decided that someone with a name as amazing as Cordelia would never toss a secret note onto someone else's desk. Cordelia would hide a secret note in a secret place. A place that only Cordelia and Anastasia will know about.

If Anastasia is clever enough to find it.

When the sidewalk is empty, I slip around back and head for the playground. I run past the swings, the slides, and the giant sandbox. I run until I come to the hogs. Actually, they're hedges that are shaped like hogs. They're hedgehogs. Get it?

Our playground has hedge animals because Mr. Benson, our custodian, is handy with hedge trimmers. We even have a dinosaur. And a ten-foot-tall giraffe.

I dodge in and out of hedge animals until I come to the cow at the sunny corner of the school. Mr. Benson hung a bell around her neck with *Bessie* painted on it.

I size up ol' Bessie for a minute.

She's grown a lot since second grade.

Since the day Jenna made Joey knock a brick out of the school.

The brick that is now hidden somewhere behind Bessie.

I get down on my hands and knees, squeeze behind her bushy body, and scoot along until I am completely hidden by her branches. I like the way she sort of hugs me all around.

I sit for awhile, wondering if anyone else has been here before. I bet not. Not unless they are a caterpillar or a toad or some other hairy, slimy thing. I check for anything hairy or slimy that might have gotten here before me. But there isn't anything. So I relax and smile a little. Because getting to be first at something, especially when it doesn't involve touching anything hairy or slimy, can make you feel pretty amazing.

I scoot closer to the school building and press my hand against the cool brick wall. I imagine all the kids on the other side getting ready for school. Sharpening their pencils. Licking down their bangs. Punching or getting punched in the arm for no apparent reason.

But not me. I'm safe, crouched behind a cow hedge. And the best part is, nobody knows it.

I start wiggling bricks, one by one, until I find the one that wiggles back. I pull it out a crack and stick my note to Anastasia in.

Then I crawl back out. Back to my old world of chewed pencils and crooked haircuts and bruised knees. I brush a leaf off my shirt, give Bessie a pat, and head inside.

All morning during class, I wait for our first recess to arrive. When it finally does, I pretend to tie my shoes until everyone leaves the classroom. Then I go to the chalkboard and find a small spot that isn't already covered with math problems and social studies questions and classroom papers and pictures Mr. Crow likes to display there. I pick up a piece of chalk and write:

Anastasia:

Then I draw:

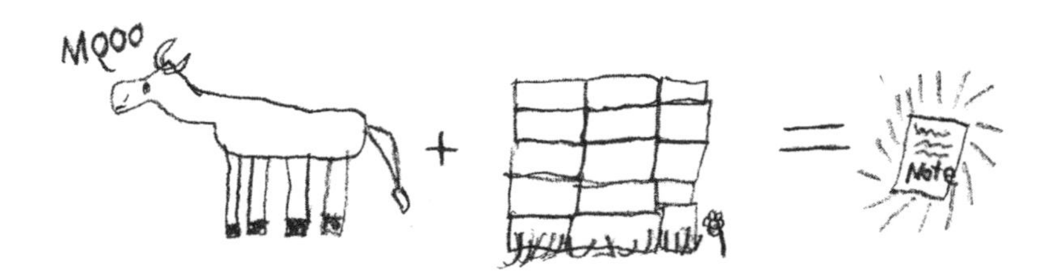

I drop the chalk and run outside.

I hope Stacey will see the message.

I double hope she is clever enough to figure it out.

I triple hope no one else is.

I sit with the other girls during lunch, but I barely eat anything. I'm too busy wondering if Stacey will see my message before the afternoon recess. Then, when it's recess, I try to keep an eye on Bessie, but I don't get too close to the hedge in case Stacey catches me hanging around it. So I mostly just wander around the playground by myself, as usual, and wait.

When the recess bell finally rings, I wait for Stacey to head back inside, and run to Bessie.

I squeeze behind her, wiggle the loose brick, and . . .

My note is gone.

I can't get to sleep that night because I keep wondering if Stacey found my note or if it got carried off by squirrels or something. And if she did find it, I wonder if she will write back to me.

"What do you think?" I ask George. "Will she?"

George is apparently sleeping, because he doesn't answer.

"Not that I'm holding my breath or anything," I say. "I mean, she's so busy running around with Jenna she'll probably forget all about the note by tomorrow. Or else she'll show it to Jenna, and Jenna will show it to everyone, and they will figure out that I'm the weird one who wrote it. Then the whole school will be calling me I-*duh,* including Stacey Merriweather."

I sigh and roll over.

"Still," I whisper. "I wouldn't mind if she wrote back."

Chapter 10

As soon as I get off the bus the next morning, I sneak behind the school. I crawl behind Bessie, even though I know Stacey probably hasn't had time to hide a note. And guess what? There's no note.

I crawl out. "I'll be back this afternoon," I tell Bessie. Then I trudge inside.

When I get to our classroom, everyone is already there. Even Jenna's mom is there. She's holding a clipboard, and there is a pencil tucked behind her ear.

The bell rings, and Mr. Crow says, "Take your seats, everyone. We have a special guest today. Please welcome our PTA president, and Jenna's mom, Mrs. Drews."

Jenna applauds.

"Thank you for that warm welcome, everyone," Jenna's mom says. "I'm here today not only as your PTA president but also as chairperson of the Purdee Potato Pageant."

"What's that?" Quinn asks. Quinn wasn't here for last year's Potato Pageant.

Jenna's mom raises an eyebrow at Quinn. Then she scans the room and says, "As *most* of you know, the Purdee Potato Pageant is our town's big fall event. Along with the Potato Parade, 'Tater Tossing Contest, and the crowning of Miss Spud, children in fourth grade are invited to paint the storefront windows of our local businesses. First prize for the most beautifully painted window is one bushel of potatoes to be divided among those working on the painting, and—"

"What's a bushel?" Rusty asks.

"A bushel is the same as four pecks," Tom says.

"What's a peck?" Randi asks next.

"The same as eight quarts," Tom explains. "Four pecks is equal to thirty-two quarts, which is equal to one bushel."

"How many potatoes is that?" Rusty asks.

"A lot," I say.

Jenna's mom gives our cluster a look. "As I was *saying*," she continues, "the winners will receive one bushel of potatoes, *and* their photographs will appear in our town's newspaper, *The Purdee Press.*"

Brooke Morgan flicks her long hair off her shoulders. "My sister, Jade, is a Miss Spud contestant," she says. "I bet we'll *both* get our pictures in the newspaper." She bats her eyes at Jenna's mom. Brooke probably figures the chairperson of the Potato Pageant gets to vote for the most beautiful window. And there's nothing Brooke likes better than seeing her picture in the newspaper.

Mr. Crow steps forward. "This will be a great project for our classroom clusters!" he says. Then he turns to Jenna's mom. "You can plan on our class painting four windows, Mrs. Drews."

"Wonderful," she says, jotting a note on her clipboard. "The Potato Pageant is on October 13th. That means you have one month to plan your window designs."

"We'll start thinking of designs now," Mr. Crow says. "And paint the windows the day before the pageant."

"I'm glad Jenna's in my cluster," Brooke says. "She's such a great artist."

Jenna nods. Brooke gives Jenna's mom her most pleasant smile. Jenna's mom smiles back and jots another note on her clipboard.

I look at the kids in my cluster. Rusty is sticking pencils up his nose. Randi is flexing her skull-and-crossbones temporary tattoo. Tom is reading the glossary in his science book.

"Can you guys paint?" I ask.

Nobody answers.

When it's time for recess, I take my sketchbook and a pencil outside with me. I sit on a bench that is nowhere near Bessie. If Stacey hides a note for me, I don't want her to see me hanging around.

I turn to a blank page and start drawing potatoes. By the time I've drawn six it's clear that there is nothing beautiful about them.

So I add faces. And clothing.

My first potato gets shaggy hair and a basketball jersey. I write *Randi* under it. I give the next potato long hair, two bright eyes, and perfectly straight teeth. Then I write *Brooke* under it. I dress the next two potatoes in matching sweaters, necklaces, and earrings. But I give one dark hair and one light hair. *Meeka* and *Jolene.*

I add several rotten spots to the next potato. I give it cross-eyes. Ten of them. And a potato bug crawling out of its nose. I write *Jenna* underneath.

There is one potato left. I give it curly hair. And a friendly smile.

"What's *that*?" I hear someone say.

I look up. Jenna Drews is standing over me, glaring at my potato people. I quickly close my sketchbook before she has time to read the names I've written under them. "Nothing," I say, and start to get up.

Jenna pushes me back down. "It looked like *potatoes* to me," Jenna sneers. Then she leans in close. "Don't even *think* about trying to win that contest, I-*duh*. Nobody knows potatoes like I do."

"Well, you are a vegetarian," I say.

Jenna plants her feet and lifts her chin. "That's right. And don't you forget it."

"Not to mention a *boss*etarian," I mumble.

"Don't you *dare*—," Jenna starts to say. But just then the bell rings and everyone starts running inside. Jenna knocks my sketchbook out of my hands and marches away. She falls in step with Stacey, shooting a look back at me. Stacey looks at me, too, and starts to wave. But Jenna grabs her hand and holds it tight.

I pick up my sketchbook and open it to the potato page. I write *Anastasia* under my last potato. Then I close the book and hope that she left a note.

When I get back to the classroom, everyone is still milling around. Mr. Crow is nowhere in sight. But Stacey Merriweather is. She's standing behind Rusty's desk, watching him play "Pirates of the Caribbean" on his hand-held. Just as I sit down, Rusty throws his hands up in the air, practically punching me in the face. "Yes!" he shouts. "It took me three days to clear that level!"

Randi reaches across her desk and gives Rusty a high five. Tom, who is reading a paperback, raises his eyebrows in a silent salute.

"I cleared that level in an hour," Stacey says. "But then, I had the cheats."

Rusty swings around and gawks at Stacey. "You've got the cheat codes for this level?"

Stacey nods. "I have the cheats for *all* the levels. In fact, I know cheats that nobody else knows about."

Now it's my turn to raise an eyebrow.

Rusty drops his jaw. "Wow," he says, all impressed. "What are they?"

Stacey pulls at the collar of her sweater like someone just cranked up the thermostat. "Um . . . well, it's not like I have them memorized," she says, inching away from Rusty.

"Can you bring them tomorrow?" Rusty asks.

"Um . . . no," Stacey says. "I don't have them anymore. I mean, I didn't bring them with to my . . . um . . . aunt's house."

Rusty slumps.

Stacey hurries back to her cluster.

Mr. Crow comes dashing into the room. "Sorry I'm late!" he says. "I was in the cafeteria."

"But lunch is still an hour away," Joey points out.

"I wasn't eating lunch," Mr. Crow says. "I was looking for these."

Mr. Crow holds up a lumpy plastic bag. He pulls a potato out of it. Then he walks around the room and gives each cluster one potato. "I thought potatoes would provide inspiration as you begin designing your Potato Pageant windows," he says. He sets a potato on Randi's desk and a sheet of drawing paper on mine.

"Ida, why don't you sketch out the ideas your group comes up with," Mr. Crow says.

I blink at Mr. Crow. "But I'm not really a take-charge kind of person," I say.

Mr. Crow pats my shoulder. "You'll do fine," he says, and walks away.

I look around my cluster. "Any ideas for a design?" I ask.

Randi picks up the potato and gives it a sniff. Then she shrugs and tosses it to Rusty. Rusty catches it and lobs it back to her. "Betcha can't throw a knuckleball," he says.

"Betcha I can," Randi replies, and digs her knuckles into the potato. Meanwhile, Tom opens his math book and begins reading the glossary.

I look at the sheet of paper Mr. Crow gave me. I remember all the goofy pictures Elizabeth and I used to draw. Then I pick up my pencil.

First, I draw a ship with tall masts and large

sails. I study Randi's fake tattoo while she pitches the potato to Rusty. Then I draw a skull and crossbones on a sail. I draw potatoes on the deck of the ship. I even plant one in the crow's nest. I put a scar on his cheek and patches over three of his eyes. I give some of the potatoes long mustaches and gold earrings. Several swing swords. One has a wooden leg. Then I draw choppy water under the ship. I use my best swirly cursive to write *Potatoes of the Caribbean* in the waves.

"That's great, Ida!"

I look up and see Mr. Crow standing over me, looking at my drawing. I cover it with one arm like I'm hiding booty.

"May I show it to the class?" he asks.

I gulp.

Mr. Crow takes that as a *yes*. He slips the picture out from under my arm and waves it around for everyone to see. "Look at Ida's drawing, everyone. This is wonderful potato humor!"

Everyone turns to look at my drawing. Several people actually laugh.

"That's really funny, Ida," Stacey says.

"Thanks," I mumble back.

Jenna rolls her eyes. "I don't see what pirates have to do with the pageant," she snips.

"It's a *potato* pageant," I say to Jenna as Mr. Crow tapes my picture to the board. "The pirates are *potatoes.*"

"Yes, but my mother said the most beautiful design will win the contest," Jenna says. "Pirates are *not* beautiful."

"Well," I say. "You *are* the expert of unbeautiful things."

Jenna gives me a scowl. A few people hold back giggles. Then she says, "If you want to see something that *is* beautiful, look at *this.*"

Jenna holds up the drawing she is working on. It's a field of potatoes. Bunnies scamper around it. Butterflies flutter over it. A rainbow stretches across the sky. It ends at the feet of a smiling girl who is wearing her hair in two braids.

Dominic glances at Jenna's picture. "*Borrr-ing,*" he whispers.

"What did you say?" Jenna snaps.

Dominic shifts in his seat. "*Beauuu-tiful*?" he offers. Then he ducks his head and pretends to be very interested in studying his potato.

Jenna gets up and practically jabs her picture into Mr. Crow's face.

"Very nice, Jenna," he says, backing away.

"Don't you want to hang it up?" Jenna asks.

"Maybe later," he says. "Right now Ida's picture is on the board."

Jenna's face heats up like a plate of french fries. She stomps back to her desk and glares at me. Then she grits her teeth and hisses, "Not. For. Long."

At lunch, everyone is talking about the Potato Pageant. But I just sit quietly and think about getting a note from Anastasia. When it's time for afternoon recess, I sneak over to Bessie and slip behind her branches when no one is looking.

I see a note hidden there.

I pull it out.

And smile.

Chapter 11

Riding home on the bus, I read the note for the twenty-ninth time.

Dear Cordelia,

This is a great hiding place! Let's keep it a secret, okay? It's fun to have a good secret for a change.

Leave the letter A on your desk so I'll know who you are. I'd really like to know. I'll keep that a secret, too.

By the way, my real name isn't Anastasia. I'm sorry I lied.

Anastasia

I wonder why she lied about her real name. I

wonder if she's lying when she says she will keep this a secret. I wonder if she lies about everything.

I wonder if I should write back.

When I get home, my mom is outside, digging in her flower bed.

"Hi, Ida!" she calls, as I walk up the driveway. She brushes dirt off her gloves and sits back on the heels of her gardening clogs. "I ran into Jenna's mom this afternoon. She mentioned the window-painting contest."

"Yes," I say, stuffing Stacey's note into my pocket. "She mentioned it to us, too."

"Sounds like a fun project for you," my mom says. "You're so good at drawing."

I just shrug. "Mr. Crow liked my drawing of potato pirates," I say.

My mom smiles. "I bet the kids liked it, too."

I think about Jenna. "Some of them did," I say, and head inside.

When I get to my room, I pull out Stacey's note and show it to George. "She wrote back," I say.

George gives me the once-over and then waits for more information.

"She's probably lying about keeping this a secret," I say. "If I tell her who I really am she'll just run off and blab to Jenna that I'm a total baby for sending her secret notes."

I read the note again. Then I pull a piece of paper out of my desk drawer. And start writing.

Dear Anastasia,

Are you as good at keeping secrets as you are at telling lies? I know you don't live with your rich aunt. I saw her and she didn't look one bit rich. Plus, rich aunts don't wear pink curlers in their hair. Grandmothers do.

If you promise not to lie to me, I promise not to tell everyone that you aren't who you say you are.

Cordelia

I read the note to George. He shudders.

"I know," I say. "But if I'm going to keep writing to her, I have to get a few things straight right from the start."

The next morning, I hide my note to Anastasia in the secret stone before school. When I get to the classroom, my *Potatoes of the Caribbean* drawing is no longer hanging on the board. It's on my desk. Torn into a million pieces.

I give Jenna a glare. She just smiles sweetly and then starts giggling with Meeka and Jolene.

I scoop up all the pieces of paper and throw them into the wastebasket. I think about throwing Jenna in, too.

I slump in my desk.

"Jenna did it," I hear someone say.

I look up. Tom Sanders is looking at me over the top of his social studies book.

"I know," I reply.

"Are you going to tell Mr. Crow?" Tom asks.

I sigh. "No."

Tom nods. "Smart move," he says. "Remember when Jenna made me drink my fake tornado in first grade?"

"Yeah," I say.

"She did that because I told on her for smashing the block tower I was building. If you tell on her about this, she'll do something even meaner to you."

Tom goes back to reading his book. "By the way, Ida, your drawing was good," he says.

"Really?" I say.

"Really," he says back.

While Mr. Crow takes attendance, I write the letter *A* on a scrap of paper. But I don't leave it on my desk like Stacey wants me to. When it's time for our milk break, I toss the *A* onto Stacey's desk when everyone is getting their cartons of milk and the cookies Mr. Crow brought for a snack.

After our first recess, I see the letter *C* on Stacey's desk. At the end of the second recess, I check the stone again.

Dear Cordelia,

You're right, I don't have a rich aunt. And I do live with my grandma. Please don't tell anyone. I promise not to lie to you anymore. I don't usually lie. Just when it's an emergency. I can't tell you about the emergency yet. It's too scary.

I'll tell you a secret, though. I think Jenna Drews is mean.

Anastasia

P.S. Why are you scared to tell me who you really are?

Chapter 12

When I get back to the classroom, it's time for Phys Ed. I slip the note into my backpack and then get in line to walk to the gym.

Our Phys Ed teacher, Ms. Stein, is waiting for us when we get there. She's dressed in her usual hooded sweatshirt and training pants. Like always, there's a whistle in her mouth. Several red rubber balls huddle around her sneakers.

"The name of the game is *dodgeball,* ladies and gentlemen," she says, clenching the whistle in her teeth.

Everyone else cheers.

"I love dodgeball," I hear Stacey say to Jenna. "I'm really good at it."

"Not as good as me," Jenna says back.

Ms. Stein makes all of us number off into two

teams. I'm glad to be on Jenna's team so she can't throw balls at me. Stacey's on Jenna's team, too.

"I'll be captain," Jenna says, while Ms. Stein starts kicking balls onto the gym floor. "Stacey, you stand next to me." Jenna positions herself front and center.

I take my usual position as far away from the line of fire as possible.

"Here, Stacey!" Jenna says, tossing a ball to her.

Stacey misses and has to chase the ball down. She finally catches it when it bumps against my feet.

"Thanks for stopping it, Ida," Stacey says.

"No problem," I reply.

"Do you want to stand up front with us?" Stacey asks.

"No," I say. "I prefer to stand in back and keep my teeth inside my head."

"Get back up here, Stacey!" Jenna yells.

Stacey picks up the ball and hurries back to the center line. She stands next to Jenna, shifting back and forth like there are thumbtacks in her sneakers.

Ms. Stein blows her whistle.

Stacey throws the ball as hard as she can. But it barely makes it across the center line. Randi snatches it up and chucks it back. It nails Stacey in the leg. She crumples to her knees.

"Gotcha, Stace!" Randi calls.

Ms. Stein blows her whistle and points to Stacey. "Benched!" she shouts.

Meanwhile, Jenna whips a ball at Jolene, knocking her out of the competition. "I thought you said you were good?" Jenna says to Stacey as she scoops up another ball.

Stacey just shrugs and limps to the sidelines. She sits down on the floor, looking relieved.

I'm so busy watching Stacey, I don't notice Quinn zeroing in on me. A ball slams into my shoulder, sending me into a death spin.

"Get off the floor before you trip someone!" Jenna yells at me.

"Aye, aye, Captain," I say, and crawl out of the game.

I sit next to Stacey. We watch the action for a few minutes, and then I hear her say, "Actually, I'm not that crazy about dodgeball."

"Actually, I'm not either," I reply.

"I'm better at individualized sports," she says. "Like dance."

"I'm better at civilized sports," I say back. "Like checkers."

It isn't long before the only people still playing are Zane and Jenna on our team and Randi on the other team.

Jenna throws a ball hard at Randi, but it whizzes past her.

Randi bullets a ball at Zane. It ricochets off his hip and hits Jenna square in the stomach. She goes down like a sack of flour.

"Gotcha!" Randi hollers. She does a little victory dance.

Ms. Stein blows her whistle. "The winners!" she shouts, pointing to Randi's team.

Jenna scrambles to her feet and gives Zane a shove.

"What was that for?" Zane asks.

"For losing the game," Jenna says, stomping off the floor.

Ms. Stein forces us to play three more games of dodgeball. For the last game, Jenna positions Stacey in back with me and moves the Dylans up front with her. Stacey doesn't seem to mind.

When I get home after school I read Stacey's note to George. "I wonder what her scary emergency is," I say. "And why she's friends with Jenna if she thinks she's mean."

I wait for George to comment. But he just stares at me with his big smile. "Maybe lying makes her feel better about the emergency," I say. "But I think she means it when she says she won't lie to me anymore."

I tuck the note away and get out my sketchbook.

I draw Stacey. And a big hairy monster with multiple eyes and large claws chasing her.

Then I draw me, pelting it with stones.

That night, when my dad is tucking me in, I say, "Dad? What are you scared of?"

My dad thinks for a minute. Then he says, "War. Tornadoes. Leather gloves."

"Leather gloves?"

My dad nods. "When I was your age, a bully at my school named Allen Bentley wore leather gloves every day of the year. He'd come up behind me on the playground, grab my neck, and squeeze until I choked. Then he'd say, 'Outta my way, May*flower,*' and push me to the ground."

"What did you do? I mean, did you tell on Allen Bentley?"

"Nope," my dad says. "Not until today." He smiles at me. "Funny, but I suddenly feel better about leather gloves."

My dad pulls the covers up to my chin. "Is there anything you want to tell me about, Ida? Anything scary?"

I think of all the scary stuff I could tell him about. Elizabeth moving away. Jenna being mean. Stacey's secret emergency. But telling him about it feels scary, too.

"No," I say. "Not tonight."

My dad gives me half a smile. "All right, then. Good night, Ida. Sleep tight."

"Same to you," I reply.

After my dad leaves, I crawl out of bed. I turn on my desk lamp and find a piece of paper and a pencil.

Dear Anastasia,

I'm not exactly scared to tell you who I really am. It just feels safer to be Cordelia for now.

But I am scared of Jenna Drews. I'm afraid her big, bossy head will explode and all her sawdust brains will shoot out and block the sun and we will have three years of endless winter.

Cordelia

P.S. If you think Jenna's so mean, why are you friends with her?

P.P.S. I'm sorry about your scary emergency. I'm glad you told me the truth about it, even if you didn't tell me what it is.

Chapter 13

The next morning I don't mind waiting for the bus, or even sitting by myself on the way to school. I know that as soon as I get there, I will hide my note for Anastasia. Which I do.

And when recess comes and Jenna pulls Stacey, Meeka, Brooke, and Jolene off to the swings, leaving me behind, I don't feel so bad, because I know that Stacey will find a way to sneak off and that later in the day I will find another note in the secret stone from her.

Which I do.

Dear Cordelia,

I made up stories about myself because I wanted to make friends fast. But now I have to keep making up new stories because I'm afraid Jenna will be mean to me if she finds out that I'm not very interesting after all.

Here's a story I started last night:

Once upon a time, two girls were lost in a deep, dark forest. They walked for hours until they came to a little lake that was shaped like a spoon. There was a sign posted by the lake with a poem that read:

Spoon of the lake,
Spoon of the sea,
Carry me off
To afternoon tea.

So the girls said the poem together and then stepped onto the lake. They floated across it and they didn't even get wet.

I love making up stories like that, don't you? What do you think should happen next?

Anastasia

There isn't time for me to answer Stacey right away. Besides, I could never write something as good as she did on short notice. So I tuck the note in my pocket and head back to class.

Since it's Thursday, we have show-and-tell. This happens once a week and we are not required to bring anything if we don't want to. And guess what? I don't.

But Brooke walks to the front of the class and places a glittery crown on her head. "This is a genuine rhinestone tiara," she brags, pointing to her head. "I won it last summer at the statewide Little Miss Showstopper contest. It would be bigger, but I came in second place because I missed one of the questions during the contest quiz."

"What question did you miss?" Randi asks.

Brooke clears her throat and pretends to speak into a microphone. "Who was the second president of the United States?"

"Easy," Jenna says. "Everyone knows it was Abraham Lincoln."

"Wasn't he the sixteenth president?" Stacey asks.

Jenna gives Stacey a look. "No," she says. "Lincoln came in second."

"Just like me!" Brooke says, tilting her tiara to catch the light. "Now, as I was saying—"

"You're wrong, Jenna," Tom interrupts. Jenna whips around and stares Tom down.

Tom gulps, but then he continues. "John Adams was the second president. Followed by Thomas Jefferson, James Madison, James Monroe—"

"All right, all right," Jenna cuts Tom off. "Nobody likes a know-it-all."

"You can say that again," I mumble.

After Brooke demonstrates the talent she performed for the contest (whistling "The Star-Spangled Banner" while tap-dancing), she waltzes back to her desk.

Quinn gets up next and shows a bird skull. "I found it last weekend," he says.

"That's nothing," Jenna butts in. "When my family went camping last summer I found an entire deer skeleton."

"That's great, Jenna," Mr. Crow says patiently. "But right now it's Quinn's turn to speak."

Jenna clamps her mouth shut and slumps back in her chair.

When Quinn is done showing his bird skull, Mr. Crow says, "Anyone else?"

Stacey slowly raises her hand. She walks up front and pulls a piece of paper out of her pocket. "This is a poem I wrote last night," she says. She takes a deep breath and begins reading from the paper.

A friend is someone special.
A friend is someone true.
A friend can make you laugh,
When you're feeling blue.
A friend is always with you,
Every hour of every day.
A friend is still a friend,
Even when you're far away.

When Stacey is done reading, everyone applauds. "Well done, Stacey!" Mr. Crow says. "May I post your poem on the board?" Stacey nods, and gives the poem to him.

She sits back down. Jenna smiles at Stacey like she wrote the poem for her.

But Stacey glances away from Jenna. And smiles down at her desk instead.

After school, I take Anastasia's note home with me and write my reply.

Dear Anastasia,

You are a really good writer. I don't write much because I'm saving my brain for middle school. But I do like to draw. So here is a picture of what I think happens next in your story.

I think for a minute and then I draw a picture of two girls riding on the back of a cow. The cow is speckled with stars and it's walking through a field of yellow daisies. Then I draw a little cottage in the distance. It's covered with moss and vines and absolutely nothing hairy or slimy.

Now it's your turn to finish the story.

Cordelia

P.S. What do you like to do when you aren't writing? Remember, you can't lie.

The next morning, I leave the note in the secret stone. Later that afternoon, I get Anastasia's reply.

Dear Cordelia,

Your drawing is great! I'm going to hang it up in my bedroom. I hope you don't mind.

Here's the rest of the story:

After the girls rode the enchanted cow to the cottage, they went inside and found a round table covered with a white lacy tablecloth. Hot tea and honey steamed in a china teapot on the table, and little plates of cookies and candies waited to be eaten. So they sat down and ate and laughed and drank tea together until evening came. Then they floated back across the spoon lake, leaving a trail of daisies behind so they could always find their way back. The End.

Don't you wish every day could be as perfect as that? I do.

Anastasia

P.S. Besides writing, I like to dance. Before I moved here I took ballet lessons. I can't take them now because everything is too messed up and my parents have to spend their money on other things. Still, I wish I could dance again.

P.P.S. What do you wish for, Cordelia?

All weekend, I think about my picture hanging in Stacey's bedroom. I also think about Elizabeth, because she used to hang my pictures up in her bedroom, too.

On Monday morning, I leave my answer to Anastasia in the secret stone.

Dear Anastasia,

I wish dodgeball would be outlawed. I wish all teachers were as nice as Mr. Crow. I wish a potato would sprout out of Jenna Drews's ear.

But mostly, I wish my best friend, Elizabeth, hadn't moved away.

Cordelia

P.S. I like the ending of your story. Someday you should write books when you aren't busy dancing.

P.P.S. What else do you wish for?

She writes back:

Dear Cordelia,

I wish friends never had to move away.

Anastasia

P.S. Look in Bessie's branches!

When I push aside one of Bessie's branches, I see a little pink plastic cup. There is a note with it that says it's a magic cup, even though I know it's really just for Barbies. The note also says:

Fill me up with wishes,
Pour them over you.
Give them time to sink in,
Then they will come true!

I tuck the magic cup into my pocket. As I do, I feel my purple gel pen in there. Even though I like it a lot, I decide Stacey might like it, too. So I pull out the pen and a piece of paper and write:

Dear Anastasia,

Thank you for the magic cup. It's the first one I've ever had. There's something for you in Bessie's branches, too. It's not exactly magical, but I thought you might like it anyway.

Cordelia

I slip the note into the secret stone. Then I hide the pen in Bessie's branches.

———

My dad has the afternoon off, so he picks me up after school and suggests we go to the park together. On the way there I say, "Dad? If you could make three wishes, what would they be?"

My dad glances at me. "Three wishes?" he says. "Let's see . . . how about . . . thirty-six hours in each day, a lifetime supply of cappuccino, and . . . three more wishes?" He concludes his wish list with a goofy grin.

"Longer days and more cappuccino?" I say. "That's the best you can do?"

My dad just shrugs and turns the car onto the street that leads to the park. "I guess I'm just happy with who I am and what I have right now," he says. "So, what about you, Ida? What do you wish for?"

I fidget a little in my seat. "I'm still working on that," I say.

When we get home from the park, I go to my room and set the magic cup by my bed. I stare at it for about three hours.

Then I make three wishes.

"I wish that I could be as smart as Tom

Sanders, as pretty as Brooke Morgan, and as good at sports as Randi Peterson."

But they are just practice wishes, which is a good thing because the cup just sits there.

It doesn't jiggle or glow.

No magic sparks.

No smoke.

No nothing.

Then I remember to pick up the cup and pour the wishes over my head. I feel kind of stupid doing it. But afterward, I feel better. Like maybe it's really working.

Then I wish my real wish. That I weren't afraid to tell Stacey who I really am.

But I don't pour that wish out. Not yet.

Chapter 14

I keep my magic cup next to my bed. Even though it doesn't jiggle or glow or do any of the usual magical stuff, I like seeing it there. And I like remembering who gave it to me.

I also like going to school because Stacey uses my purple gel pen to write me more notes. I write notes to her, too. Plus, I draw more pictures. By the time two weeks have gone by, I've drawn her three magical cows, two ballet dancers, and one smiling monkey. I don't know how she has time to keep checking the secret stone with Jenna always around, but I'm glad she does.

Then, before school one Friday morning, I check the secret stone and find this note from her.

Dear Cordelia,

I couldn't wait to tell you! My mom called

last night and she's coming to see me this weekend. We're going to a movie and out to eat and everything. I'm going to show her all the pictures you gave me. I know she'll like them. I told her about the story we wrote together. She said it made her sad that the girls were lost in the forest. But she was glad they had each other.

What are you doing this weekend?

Anastasia

I pull a piece of paper out of my backpack and write my reply.

Dear Anastasia,

I'm glad you get to see your mom. Is your dad busy traveling? My dad will be traveling this weekend, too, so me and my mom will probably cook stuff he doesn't like to eat and watch movies that make him yawn.

I bet you miss your parents when they're away. I know I do. I miss Elizabeth, too, even though I'm starting to get used to her being gone.

Cordelia

Later that morning, during silent reading, I overhear Jenna whispering to Stacey.

"But why can't you go to a movie this weekend?"

Stacey fidgets behind her book. "Um . . . because my aunt and I have something planned."

"So?" Jenna says. "Skip it."

Stacey turns a page in her book and whispers, "I can't."

Jenna huffs and snaps her book shut.

Later that afternoon, I find another note in the secret stone.

Dear Cordelia,

Actually, my dad doesn't travel very much. Neither does my mom. I miss them a lot, even though I like living with my grandma. She tries to make me laugh every day.

I miss my old friends, too. Especially Kate. She was funny, like you. One time, at lunch, she told a joke and I laughed so hard milk came out of my nose! I don't recommend trying this.

Write to me next week!

Anastasia

I think about the note from Anastasia while I help my mom get supper ready that night. As I chop up a green pepper for tacos, I say, "Mom? I need a good joke. One that will make someone really laugh."

My mom thinks for a minute while she drains a can of black olives. Then she says, "Why did the chicken cross the road?"

"Why?" I ask.

"To get to the other side," she replies.

I roll my eyes. "That's the oldest joke in the world, Mom."

My mom just shrugs. "Better ask your dad when he calls tonight. He's the joke expert."

Later, when the phone rings, I answer it. It's my dad calling from his hotel.

"So what have you and Mom been up to?" he asks.

"We made tacos with green peppers and black olives," I say.

"Sorry I asked," he says back. "What else?"

"We watched a movie about this lady who goes to the grocery store to buy pork chops and ends up falling in love with her butcher."

My dad yawns.

When he's done yawning, I say, "Dad? I need a joke."

"What kind of joke?" he asks.

"Any kind," I say. "For someone who needs a laugh."

My dad is quiet. Then he asks, "Is this someone a friend from school?"

I think for a moment. "Sort of," I say.

My dad is quiet again. Then he clears his throat and says, "Why did the taco cross the road?"

I sigh. "Don't you mean *chicken*?"

"Nope," he says. "Taco."

"Okay," I say. "Why did the *taco* cross the road?"

I can practically see my dad's goofy grin as he replies, "It was taped to the chicken."

I roll my eyes. "Sorry I asked," I say.

My dad laughs.

Just before I go to bed, I write my note to Anastasia.

Dear Anastasia,
Here's a joke for you. (I hope you aren't drinking milk.)

Why did the taco cross the road?
Answer: It was taped to the chicken.

So it isn't the best joke. I hope it makes you laugh anyway.

Cordelia

P.S. Your grandma sounds nice.

P.P.S. I think it's better to have a nice grandma than a rich aunt.

On Monday morning, I hide the note in the secret stone. When I get inside the school, Jenna, Brooke, Meeka, and Jolene are giggling in the hallway. They don't even notice when I walk past them.

I go into the classroom. Randi and some of the boys are playing a game on the computer. Mr. Crow is writing the week's schedule on the board. He's already written *Math quiz* and *Book reports due* under *Tuesday* and *Thursday.* Under *Friday* he writes *Paint pageant windows.*

Stacey isn't around, so I hurry and find a scrap of paper in my desk. I write the letter *A* on it. I think about the chicken joke I wrote for her. And draw a dancing chicken under the *A.*

I toss the paper onto her desk just as the bell

rings. Jenna, Brooke, Meeka, and Jolene pile into the classroom. Stacey piles in, too.

"So that's my plan," Jenna says to the others. "You spend the night at my house on Friday and we all go to the Potato Parade together on Saturday."

"I'll have to ask if it's okay," Meeka says.

"Me, too," Jolene adds.

Jenna narrows her eyes. "Just *tell* your parents you have to spend the night. Say we're getting ready for the window-painting contest."

Meeka and Jolene nod obediently. Brooke nods, too. Stacey is about to nod, but then she glances at me. I pull my math book out of my desk and pretend to be very interested in long division.

"What about Ida?" I hear Stacey whisper to Jenna.

"What about her?" Jenna asks.

"Aren't you going to invite her, too? And Randi?"

"This party is for my *best* friends," Jenna says.

"But—," Stacey starts to say.

"Besides," Jenna interrupts, glancing over her shoulder at me, "you're busy this weekend, aren't you, I-*duh*."

I glance up from my book. "Yes, Jenna," I say. "If you're planning a sleepover, I'm busy."

"See?" Jenna says, as she herds the others to her cluster. "She can't come."

Stacey is about to say something back to Jenna, but then she sees the dancing chicken on her desk.

"What's that?" Jenna asks.

"Oh, it's nothing," Stacey says, crumpling up the paper. "Just a . . . a note."

I gulp.

"A *note*?" Jenna says. "Who from?"

"A boy, I bet," Jolene says. Meeka giggles and nods.

"No, it's not from a boy," Stacey says. "It's from . . . um . . . my aunt."

"Your *aunt*?" Jenna says, grabbing the note from Stacey and uncrumpling it.

Stacey nods. "See?" she says, pointing to the note. "The *A* stands for *Aunt*."

Jenna gives Stacey a look. "Then what does the dancing chicken stand for?" she asks.

"Um . . . it's a secret code for . . . for . . ."

"For what?" Jenna persists.

"For *it's none of your business*," I hear myself mumble.

Jenna whips around so fast her braids fly off her shoulders. Meanwhile, Stacey snatches the note from her hand and hurries with it to the wastebasket.

Brooke, Jolene, and Meeka slip quietly away. But Jenna just stands there, glaring at me. "From her *aunt,* huh?" she finally says. "I bet."

I see the letter *C* on Stacey's desk right after our second recess. Jenna didn't let Stacey out of her sight all day, so I don't know how she managed to get my note and hide one for me. But right after school I run to the secret stone and find one.

Dear Cordelia,

Thanks for the joke! It did make me laugh. Here's a poem for you:

There once was a girl named Cordelia,
Who had a delicious i-dee-lia.
She cooked up a pot,
Of beans, spicy hot,
Then put them inside a tor-tee-lia!

Ha-ha.

Anastasia

P.S. My grandma is the best!

P.P.S. I think it's better to have a secret friend than a mean friend.

As I read Anastasia's poem, I notice there are little stars around *Cordelia,* just like the stars I painted on the whale rock I left at Jenna's house. I wonder what happened to that rock. Jenna probably uses it for target practice on Rachel.

I also notice that Stacey calls me her secret *friend.*

I wonder if secret friends can be best friends, too.

Chapter 15

I stuff Anastasia's note into my backpack and hurry to the bus. I climb on and scan the crowd for an empty seat. I see one about halfway back. *My lucky day,* I say to myself.

I start pushing toward it, but then I feel a tug on my sleeve.

I look down.

Rachel Drews is smiling up at me. "Hi, Queen Cordelia," she says.

"Hi, Princess Penelope," I say back.

"Sit here," Rachel says, scooting over.

Even though Jenna will probably call me a baby for sitting up front, I sit down next to Rachel. "Seen any monsters lately?" I ask.

Rachel giggles. "Yep," she says. "Lots."

"Me, too," I say.

"Guess what?" Rachel says.

"What?" I say back.

"Jenna's having another sleepover."

"So I've heard."

"Are you coming?" Rachel asks.

"Um, no," I say. "I have other plans."

"Like what?"

"Like staying home and cleaning my room," I say.

Rachel gives me a puzzled look. Then she says, "Didn't Jenna invite you?"

I glance away. "Not exactly," I say.

Rachel gives me a nod. "She didn't exactly invite me, either," she says.

While we wait for the last few kids to get on the bus, Rachel introduces me to the zippers on her backpack. "I named this one Joyce and this one Joyce Junior," she explains, pointing to a long zipper on top of her bag and a shorter one down the side.

"What about that one?" I ask, pointing to a chunky green zipper on one of the bag's many pockets.

"That's Max," she says. Then she leans in and

whispers, "He gets jealous if I zip Joyce more than him." She demonstrates by giving Joyce a tug. Then she gives Max two.

We sit there, contemplating zippers for a moment. Then Rachel says, "Guess what, Ida? I get to ride on a float in the Potato Parade."

"Wow," I say. "You must be famous."

"Yep. So is my mom. She's the Potato Pageant chairperson. We get to throw candy and everything!"

"I'm glad you won't be throwing potatoes," I say.

Rachel giggles. "I'll throw candy to you, Ida," she says. "Lots."

"Thanks," I say. "I can use it."

Just as the bus driver is about to close the door, Jenna scrambles on. When she sees me sitting with Rachel, she pauses to give me a disgusted look. "A kindergartener?" she says. "That's the best you can do for a friend?"

I look up at Jenna. "I thought I'd start small," I say.

Rachel smiles at me. Then she looks at her sister. "Maybe you should start small, too, Jenna."

Jenna shoots a look at Rachel. "I don't need to start anywhere," she snaps. "I already have *tons* of friends."

"Then how come you never get invited to their houses?" Rachel asks.

For a second Jenna looks like someone socked her in the stomach. Then she pulls herself together and says, "I *do*. But they would rather come to *my* house." She quickly pushes past us. And lands in the empty seat halfway back.

"No, they wouldn't," Rachel says to me. "They only come to our house because they're afraid of getting slugged if they don't show up."

"How do you know?" I ask.

Rachel shrugs. "I just do," she says.

I nod. "I just do, too," I say.

When we get off at our bus stop, Rachel waves good-bye to me. "See you at the parade, Ida!" she calls, as Jenna grabs her arm and drags her away.

When I get home, I go to my room, get out my sketchbook, and draw a picture of Princess Penelope. I give her a sparkly crown. And a pile of ammunition.

George suggests I give the picture to Rachel the next time I see her.

"Smart monkey," I say, and tear it out of my sketchbook. I fold it up and put it in my backpack.

Then I get out my note from Anastasia. I read the poem again. I pull a piece of paper out of my desk drawer and write a note back.

Dear Anastasia,

Thanks for the poem. Now I'm craving tacos. Too bad we aren't getting ready to celebrate the Purdee Taco Pageant together. They'd print your poem in the newspaper for sure. Plus, a Taco Tossing Contest sounds much more exciting than a 'Tater Tossing Contest. And then the pageant queen could be crowned The Big Enchilada.

Cordelia

P.S. I hope you have fun at the parade this weekend. Watch out for flying potatoes.

After supper I do my homework while my mom reads the newspaper. When she's done, I find scissors and a glue stick. I cut out the letters

H, *I*, and *A* from the headlines. Then I glue them to a piece of notebook paper so they say *HI A*.

I tuck the message inside my backpack, along with Rachel's picture.

The next morning when I get to the bus stop, Jenna is already there, talking Quinn's ear off. Rachel and Tess are standing together comparing shoelaces. I walk over to Rachel and hand her the folded up picture of Princess Penelope. "Better save it for later," I whisper, glancing at Jenna.

Rachel gives me a knowing nod. She unzips Joyce and puts the picture inside her backpack. Then she zips Max twice.

When I get to school, I leave my note in the secret stone. I slip my newspaper message under some graded papers Mr. Crow has put on Stacey's desk.

After our first recess, I see Stacey in the coatroom, digging around in her lunch box. She pulls out a juice box of Hi-C, carries it into the classroom, and sets it on the edge of her desk.

"What's that for?" Jenna asks her.

Stacey does a fake cough. "Scratchy throat," she says, pointing to her neck.

But the Hi-C just sits there, so I know it's really a secret message to me.

Later, when I check the secret stone, I find this note from Anastasia:

Dear Cordelia,

Jenna wants me to go to the parade with her, but I know my grandma will be there. If we run into her I will have to explain to Jenna that she isn't my rich aunt. And then my grandma will feel sad that I told lies about her. And Jenna will be mad that I lied to her, too.

Maybe I'll pretend to be sick so I don't have to go.

Anastasia

It's cold and drizzly as I walk home from the bus stop. A bike is parked by our door, and when I get inside I hear some kid plunking on the piano. The notes don't match at all.

I head to my room and close the door tight, shutting out the sound. George gives me a grateful look from my bed.

I just shake my head at him. "Too lazy to get up and close the door?"

No response from the monkey. I walk over to George and pick him up. "You have to learn to do some things for yourself, you know."

George just stares at my left ear. But I can tell he's listening. "If you sit around and wait for me to solve your problems, you will start to collect dust. And dust attracts *moths,* George. Big ones."

I sit down at my desk and set George on my lap. I pull out some paper and start writing.

Dear Anastasia,

I think if Jenna were a real friend, she would want to know the truth about you living with your grandmother. And she wouldn't be mean about it. Besides, you can't pretend to be sick forever. And you can't lie forever, either.

Cordelia

I plan to hide my note in the secret stone the next morning, but it's pouring rain. It's still raining when our first recess rolls around, so Mr. Crow says, "I suggest you use this time to finalize your plans for the Potato Pageant windows. We'll be painting them the day after tomorrow."

Since Jenna tore up my first design, Mr. Crow gives my cluster a new piece of paper. And since nobody in my cluster mentions the first design, I figure they weren't that crazy about potato pirates after all.

We stare blankly for awhile.

"Any ideas?" I finally ask.

"Nope," Rusty says. "My brain is fried."

Randi snickers. "French fried?"

"With ketchup on top," Tom adds, poking a finger at Rusty's red hair.

Rusty makes a fake frown. "Knock it off," he says. "Or I'll *mash* you!"

Tom makes a sly grin. "Like I'm afraid of a potato brain," he says.

Rusty grabs Tom in a headlock. "You asked for it!" he shouts, and pretends to pound Tom. Tom howls. Randi snorts. I laugh.

"Keep it down over there!" Jenna yells from her cluster. "You sound like a bunch of bawling babies."

I turn to Jenna. "Not babies," I say. "Tater Tots."

Tom finally escapes Rusty's headlock, but we still can't think of anything to draw on our paper.

"Finish up, please," Mr. Crow says. "It's almost time for art."

"You think of a design, Ida," Tom says. "You're the best artist."

"I am?" I ask.

Tom nods. Randi and Rusty nod, too.

I fidget a little and glance around the room, wishing Elizabeth would magically appear. She'd think of a clever design in about three seconds. But the only people I see are Rusty, Randi, Tom, Quinn, Dominic, Zane, Mr. Crow, Brooke, Joey, Meeka, Jolene, the Dylans, Stacey, and, of course, Jenna.

I look at the paper again. "Maybe we should draw us," I say.

"Us?" Randi, Tom, and Rusty say together.

"You know, our class." I think about the potato people I drew in my sketchbook. "We can draw potatoes . . . a bushel of them," I say. "And then we can draw everyone's faces on them."

Rusty laughs. "Yeah, and we can call it *A Bushel of Buttheads.*"

"Not that," Tom says. "Something nicer, like *A Bushel of . . .*"

"*Friends?*" Randi suggests.

"Yeah, that's good," Rusty says. "*A Bushel of Friends.*"

Tom nods. "Let's do it."

And before I know what's happening, Tom, Randi, and Rusty are drawing potatoes on our paper. So I start drawing, too. And then we decide which potato looks like which person in our class. And we add the details. And goofy names like *Tom Tater, Mashed Meeka,* and *Stacey Spud.* And we joke around and laugh and I actually have a good time.

After we draw our whole class (including *Mr. Scare Crow*), I write *A Bushel of Friends* along the bottom of the paper, and it almost seems like it's true.

Randi grabs our design and holds it up for everyone to see.

"Impressive," Mr. Crow says.

Almost everyone agrees.

Chapter 16

By the time lunch is over the rain has stopped. During second recess I hide my note for Stacey. Then I leave the letter *A* on her desk so she will know to check the secret stone before she goes home after school.

That night I tell George all about my cluster's design for the Potato Pageant window. "Even if it doesn't win, it was still fun planning it," I say.

I roll over and hug George tight. "Actually, I hope Stacey's window wins. Even if that means Jenna wins, too. I bet winning the contest would make Stacey happy. And her grandma would be proud. And maybe her mom and dad would come to see the window. I know that would make Stacey *really* happy."

I close my eyes and imagine Stacey standing in

front of the winning window, a sack of potatoes slung over her shoulder. She's smiling and the cameras are flashing.

Just thinking about her feeling happy makes me feel happy, too.

When I get to school the next morning, I check the secret stone for a note from Stacey. But there's nothing there. "She must have gotten my note yesterday," I say to myself. "Which means I better get out of here before she shows up with a note to hide."

I hurry into the school. But when I get to our hallway, I'm surprised to see Stacey is already there, talking with Brooke and Jenna outside our classroom. I wonder why she didn't leave a note for me.

I plan to walk past them, like always, but as soon as Stacey sees me she stops talking. Tears fill her eyes and then roll down her cheeks. She takes off running to the girls' bathroom.

I turn to Brooke and Jenna. "What's wrong with Stacey?" I ask.

Brooke shrugs. "Beats me," she says. "One minute we were talking, and the next minute she was crying."

"She's probably just upset because she can't come to my sleepover tomorrow night," Jenna says.

"Why not?" I ask.

"She was about to tell me, but then she saw *you* and started bawling," Jenna says. "You have such a way with friends, I-*duh*. First Eliza*butt* moves away and now Stacey *runs* away."

I'm too worried about Stacey to pay any attention to Jenna's insult. "What should we do?" I ask.

"Stay out of it," Jenna tells me. "I'll fix everything so she can come to my sleepover. In the meantime, *leave her alone*."

Jenna shoves past me and heads into the classroom. Brooke follows her. But I just stand there, trying to decide what to do. All I can think of is to run after Stacey.

Stacey is sniffling by one of the sinks in the girls' bathroom. I walk over to another sink and start washing my hands while I build up my courage to ask her why she is crying. It doesn't take me long, because I don't have much courage to build up.

"Um . . . why are you crying, Stacey?"

Stacey's bottom lip starts to quiver and her eyes fill up with tears again. "I'm crying because I have to move away. Again."

"Move away? What? Why? Where?"

Stacey wipes the tears from her cheeks and says, "My parents aren't really traveling, Ida. They don't even have important jobs. The truth is, they got divorced. My dad and my brother moved away. My mom has been staying with friends while she looks for a new place to live. She called last night to say that she found one. She's coming to get me this weekend."

Suddenly, I realize. This is the emergency Stacey wrote about.

The next thing I know, I'm running down the hallway. I run all the way to the nurse's office.

"I have to . . . have to go home. Don't feel good," I say between sobs.

Twenty minutes later, my mom is there to pick me up and take me home.

As soon as we get to our house, I run to my room and shut the door. I fall onto my bed, pull George close, and cry and cry and cry.

By the time I hear my mom knocking on my door I'm crying so hard I can't tell her to come in. She comes in anyway. She sits next to me. She doesn't say a word. She just strokes my hair and rubs my back while all my tears sink deep into my pillow.

Finally, she quietly says, "Do you want to tell me what's wrong?"

And even though it's hard to do, I tell her. I tell her how much I miss Elizabeth. And how I never even said good-bye to her. I tell her how much I like Stacey. And how she is moving away, just like Elizabeth did.

"What do you think we should do?" she asks.

I just take deep quivery breaths and shake my head.

My mom smiles softly and wipes away my tears. Then she says, "You did a very brave thing, Ida. Telling me how sad you feel. Do you think you're brave enough to tell Stacey how you feel? To tell her good-bye?"

I don't say anything. I just sit there, wondering if I am. Brave enough.

I look around my room. It doesn't look like the

room of a particularly brave girl. No bold colors. No shiny trophies. No gold crowns.

I look at my bulletin board and see a picture I drew of Elizabeth and me.

Then I look at my nightstand, see the little wishing cup Stacey gave me, and think about the last wish I put inside it.

I take a deep breath.

And pour it over my head.

Chapter 17

It takes me all morning to write the note.

Telling someone your real name just when they are moving away is hard to do. And it's even harder to imagine being best friends with someone you can't even see. But, in fourth grade, you have to start doing the hard stuff.

Dear Stacey,

I'm really glad you get to move back with your mom. I'm sure she misses you ten times more than you miss her. But I'm really sad, too. Because I don't think there's a times table big enough to figure out how much I'll miss you.

I was wondering if maybe we could be friends?

Not just secret friends but best friends?

If the answer is YES, please check the YES box below. If the answer is NO please check the NO box.

☐ YES ☐ NO

Ida May

After my mom and I eat lunch, I convince her that I feel good enough to go back to school for the afternoon. As soon as she drops me off, I run to the playground. I crawl behind Bessie and stick the note in the secret stone.

Only it doesn't seem so secret anymore.

Even though Mr. Crow is glad to see that I'm feeling better, everyone else is too busy hanging around Stacey to notice me. Everyone except Jenna, that is. Stacey must have told her the truth about why she's moving away. Now Jenna knows Stacey lied to her. She's sitting at her desk, steaming.

When it's time to line up for music, I scribble the letter *A* on a scrap of paper. But I can't toss it on Stacey's desk because Jenna's eyes are glued to me. A moment later she's in my face.

"Did you know about this?" she hisses at me.

I know she means Stacey. I don't want to lie to

Jenna, but I don't exactly want to tell her the truth, either. So I just shrug and say, "She told me this morning."

Jenna's jaw tightens and she gives Stacey a hard glare. "Why would she tell *you* and not *me*?" she asks.

"Maybe because I asked," I say, and get in line.

For a second I don't think I will be able to get the letter *A* to Stacey. But then I notice Tom is standing right in front of me, so I give him a nudge and whisper, "Will you give this to Stacey for me? But don't tell her who it's from, okay?" I fold the scrap of paper in half and hold it out to Tom.

On the way to the music room I see him catch up to Stacey and stick the paper in her hand.

When I get home that afternoon, I go straight to my mom's sewing basket. I need some embroidery thread so I can make a friendship bracelet for Stacey. I decide if she answers *yes* to my note I'll give it to her.

But if she answers *no* I'll use it to tie my lips shut. That way, I will never be able to ask anyone to be my best friend again. Ever.

I dig to the bottom of the basket. I find five spools of thread, eight buttons, and one very sharp needle. Ouch.

But no embroidery thread.

I go to find my mom. I ask her if she has any thread. And a Band-Aid.

She wraps a Band-Aid around my finger and tells me to look in her sewing basket, but to be careful of the needles.

I decide to search the house instead. George comes along as backup.

We look in every drawer. We look under every bed. We look in every closet. We find three socks, one baby tooth, and lots of lint. But no embroidery thread. Not one single strand.

"Oh well," I say to George. "No thread, no bracelet. That's that."

George gives me a very serious look.

"Stacey might say *no*," I point out. "And I'm pretty sure getting turned down feels a lot worse than giving up."

George just grits his teeth.

I stare at those monkey teeth. They give me an idea.

I hurry to the bathroom and look in the cabinet under the sink. I dig behind shampoo bottles and aftershave lotion.

Then I find it.

Bingo.

Dental floss.

Tons of it. When your dad is an orthodontist there is always a ten-year supply of dental floss in your house.

I sift through the little plastic containers. There is green mint, white waxless, red cinnamon, pink bubble gum, purple grape, and yellow banana. Six colors in six refreshing flavors. Perfect.

I scoop them up and run to my bedroom.

Then I start yanking.

I yank and yank and yank.

I tie the strands together at one end and pull the Band-Aid off my finger. I use it to stick the floss to my bedpost.

Then I start making knots, just like Elizabeth taught me.

Well, sort of like Elizabeth taught me. It had been a long time since she showed me how to make a friendship bracelet, and dental floss was never mentioned. The only thing I do remember her mentioning is to think good thoughts while you make one. She said the good thoughts will stay with the bracelet.

So each time I twist and turn and pull and tug I think of something good. Like Choco-chunks. And drawing a really great picture. Making up stories. And being able to say a proper good-bye to a real friend before it's too late.

When I'm all out of floss and good thoughts, I hold the bracelet up and turn it around and around.

Then I sigh. It looks like something you scrape off the bottom of your shoe. Not like something you give to your best friend.

But it smells good.

That's something.

Chapter 18

The next morning I crunch behind the school. By the sound of things Mr. Benson will have to start raking leaves soon.

Crunch, crunch, crunch . . .

I reach into my pocket and touch the friendship bracelet. It feels warm and bumpy against my fingers. It feels good. Better than it looks. And I feel good, too. Better than I have felt in a long time.

Crunch, crunch, crunch . . .

I walk past the hedgehogs and past the hedgeasaurus. I hurry past the giraffe. It's the last hedge before Bessie. Before the secret stone. Before Stacey's answer.

Crunch, crunch . . . crunch.

I stop and stare.

I can see the secret stone through Bessie's branches. I can see that it's empty.

My note is gone. Stacey didn't even leave a *no.* She didn't leave anything at all.

I feel the friendship bracelet slip back into my pocket.

I feel my heart slip into my socks.

I feel a sadness simmer somewhere in between.

Crunch, crunch, crunch . . .

Something is crunching, but it isn't me.

I look up.

Jenna Drews steps around the corner of the school.

"Hey, I-*duh,*" she says with a smirk. "Looking for *this*?" She pulls a piece of paper from her pocket. It's my note to Stacey!

I wheeze.

Jenna lifts her chin. "I told you to leave her alone, but you just wouldn't listen."

She takes a few steps toward me, holding the note out on the palm of her hand. "I read it," she tells me. "Stacey says she wouldn't be your best friend if you were the last doofus on earth!" Then she crumples the note up in her tight fist.

I dive for the note. I dive so hard that I knock Jenna right off her feet. I land on top of her and the note flies into Bessie's branches. Jenna shoves me away and we both scramble for it.

But Jenna is quicker than me. She grabs the note out of the branches and shoves it into her pocket. Then she rolls onto her back, sneering. "Bye-bye, best friend," she says.

I jump up. I punch my fists into my hips and yell, "Jenna Drews, if you weren't so mean, you might actually have some *real* friends! The only reason Brooke, Meeka, and Jolene hang around is because they're afraid of you! Everyone knows it's true. Even your little sister has figured it out."

Jenna just glares at me. But I don't stick around long enough to glare back. I turn and run.

I run and I run, but I'm not running away.

I'm running *to.*

To school.

To Mr. Crow's classroom.

To Stacey Merriweather.

When I get to our classroom, Stacey is sitting at her desk.

I take a deep breath and walk over to her.

"This is for you," I say. I wipe tears off my cheeks and hold the friendship bracelet in her direction.

Stacey stares at me. "Ida . . . what happened?"

"I'm okay," I say. "I just wanted to . . . give this to you . . . before you leave. It's just . . . take it . . . Stacey. Please . . . take it?"

I hold the bracelet out again, and this time Stacey takes it from my hand.

"Thanks," she says softly, and slips the bracelet on her wrist. She turns it around and around. "I've never had a friendship bracelet like this before," she says, hesitantly.

Then she smells it.

And smiles.

"But I've never had a friend like you before either . . . *Cordelia.*"

I'm quiet for a moment. Then I say, "So you did read my note."

Stacey nods. Then she reaches into her pocket and pulls out a grayish rock, knobby on one side and flat on the other. "This is for you," she says, swimming the rock through the air to my hand.

I look at that rock. It has a tail, fin, and smiling face painted on it. Then I turn it over and read *Cordelia* on the back.

Stacey gives me half a smile. "I hope you don't mind I kept it. I didn't think you wanted it, so I took it home with me. I guess it really is magical because it found you again."

I look at Stacey. "You knew it was me writing those notes all along?"

Stacey nods. "I saw *Cordelia* written on the back of the rock when I got home from the sleep-over. When I got your first note, I figured that you were her."

"Why didn't you tell me you knew?"

Stacey is quiet for a moment. Then she says, "Because I knew I'd be moving away soon. And I was afraid you wouldn't want to be my friend if I told you the truth about everything."

I think about this for a moment. Then I hold the whale rock out to Stacey.

"Here," I say. "You keep the whale. Maybe it will help you find friends at your new school."

"Thanks," Stacey says. "But I won't be needing new friends."

I give Stacey a puzzled look. "Why not?" I ask.

"When my mom called last night, I told her how much I like it here. Then she and my grandma talked for a long time. They decided I could keep living here until my mom finds a place close by. In the meantime, she'll come see me on the weekends."

I can hardly believe it's true. "This isn't one of your emergency lies, is it?" I ask.

"Of course not," Stacey says, crossing her heart. "Secret friends never lie."

Then I take a deep breath, squeeze my whale rock for luck, and say, "Stacey? I wish we could be more than just secret friends. I wish we could be real friends . . . maybe even best friends?"

I bite my lip and think about my little magic cup. I hope it's jumping around like crazy.

Stacey raises one eyebrow. "Didn't you get my answer to your last note?" she asks.

"Not . . . exactly . . . ," I say, thinking about what Jenna told me it said.

"Oh," Stacey says. "Well, my answer is *yes*! In fact, I thought we already were best friends."

I smile. A big smile.

And that's when I know, in fourth grade, wishes do come true. Maybe not all of them, but the really important ones do.

Epilogue

Even though I hate to admit it, fourth grade is actually turning out to be a lot of fun. Oh sure, it's turning out to be a lot of other things, too. It's a lot of erasing and a lot of stomachaches and a lot of feeling like you'd rather just stay in bed for the rest of your life. But now that I've lived through a couple months of it, I'd have to say that fourth grade is mostly okay.

Fourth grade means coming in second place in the Potato Pageant window-painting contest. Joey, Jolene, and the Dylans came in first. They painted their window to look like a house, and when you peeked inside one of the house's windows you saw a toy television and a toy couch with two potatoes sitting on it. Couch potatoes. Get it?

But I was feeling so happy about Stacey not

moving away that I didn't care if another cluster won the contest. Besides, me, Randi, Rusty, and Tom had lots of fun painting our window. And the second-place prize was a jumbo box of Choco-chunks for each of us. I'll take chocolate over potatoes any day.

Fourth grade means learning how to make a three-point shot. Randi Peterson is teaching me at recess. Most of the time I miss the basket. But when I do make a shot, Randi does a little victory dance, which makes it hard not to feel like a winner.

Fourth grade also means getting a new best friend. Because even though Stacey Merriweather would rather write stories than draw pictures, and even though she prefers Swiss cheese to mild cheddar, she still is. My best friend. Best friends don't have to be exactly alike or even be together every day. They just need to be there for each other when it really matters.

Plus, fourth grade means learning to expect the unexpected. I know because even though I never thought I would be brave enough to make a new best friend, I am. And even though I never expected to find what I did on my desk a few days after I told Stacey my real name, I did.

When I got to school that day, there was a wrinkly piece of paper on my desk. Actually, it was a wrinkly note. The same note I had left in the secret stone for Stacey. The note Jenna stole.

Besides the part that I had written, there was a big purple *X* from Stacey in the *yes* box. That made me smile. I guess she really wasn't lying when she said she wants to be my best friend, even before I gave her the friendship bracelet.

But there was something else on that note.

At the very bottom, in teeny-tiny print, I saw it:

Sorry.

Stacey hadn't written it because it wasn't purple. But I knew who had.

Jenna Drews.

And right away there was something else I knew, too. If Jenna can start small, with a *sorry,* maybe she can have a real friend some day.

There's still a lot of fourth grade left, but I think I'll probably make it through okay, even though I haven't gotten any smarter since it started.

But I do have a loose tooth.

That's something.